About the Author

Dr Gerard Womack has enjoyed a career as a nuclear scientist. In addition to his full-time work, he co-wrote a book on electrochemistry and a book on the physics of the interaction of high-temperature gases with powerful magnetic fields. He also co-edited a book on the engineering aspects of magnetohydrodynamics. He now lives in Worcestershire with his wife, Maureen. *The Land of Emeralds* is his second novel following his romantic-historic novel, *It all Began in Warsaw*.

The Land of Emeralds

Gerard J Womack

The Land of Emeralds

Olympia Publishers
London

www.olympiapublishers.com
OLYMPIA PAPERBACK EDITION

A CIP catalogue record for this title is
available from the British Library.

ISBN: 978-1-78830-752-9

This is a work of fiction.
Names, characters, places and incidents originate from the writer's
imagination. Any resemblance to actual persons, living or dead, is
purely coincidental.

First Published in 2021

Olympia Publishers
Tallis House
2 Tallis Street
London
EC4Y 0AB
Printed in Great Britain

Dedication

To my wife, Maureen, for her patience, help and encouragement.

Prologue

Historical setting.

The geography of the world is interesting and fascinating; especially that period known to historians as the European Age of Discovery – the age of the exploration of the world both westwards to the Americas and eastwards to Asia. It was the start of what we now call globalization – when the world seemed to shrink – becoming more accessible to all. For the first time, newly invented navigational methods and techniques allowed the seas to be explored with confidence; providing opportunities for explorers to sail away into the unknown, across unexplored oceans to discover what the world might hold. The Spanish and Portuguese were certainly intrigued, and in the fifteenth century, the conquistadores – knights and soldiers – explored westwards, and to their surprise found a whole new continent now known as the Americas – named after the Italian explorer Amerigo Vespucci who realized that Christopher Columbus had probably discovered a new continent when he sailed into the Caribbean Sea and set foot on Venezuelan soil – after first siting the Bahamian Islands.

Seemingly continental Europeans were unaware that as early as the eleventh century the Vikings had already discovered this same continent – after voyaging across the top of the world to Greenland and then on to *Vinland*, their name for North America.

There then followed a succession of Spanish and Portuguese immigrants; the innocent start of what eventually became the Hispanic colonization of Central and South America. Inevitably, political leaders soon became involved; changing this originally peaceful immigration of the good citizens of the Iberian Peninsula into a political appropriation of foreign lands – lands rightly belonging to its indigenous peoples. The politicians soon realized this new world contained a great natural wealth of, diamonds, emeralds, silver and gold. Colonization took place remarkably quickly, as can be seen by the recognition that the Portuguese explorer Ferdinand Magellan, who was the first to circumnavigate the world thus proving that it was round, was only born in 1480, and yet by 1540 most of Central and South America had been colonialized, principally by Spain and Portugal. However, this was not to last, and less than three centuries later, in 1810, Mexico declared its independence, attainting it in 1821. No doubt, it was the French Revolution at the end of the eighteenth century and the gaining of independence of most of North America, from the British, in the middle of that same century, that inspired the move to home rule for the whole of the Americas. By the end of the early part of the nineteenth century, all the Central American nations had declared themselves independent, and after little more than two centuries of colonial rule, the nations of Guatemala, El Salvador, Honduras, Nicaragua, and Costa Rica gained freedom from Europe. Colombia received independence on the 20th of July 1810.

Ominously, this decolonization was not as good as it seemed at first sight, for it encompassed the most unequal distribution of land possible, benefiting only a few landowners. The prime areas of the lands of Central and South America were now occupied by a small privileged number of European immigrants; whilst by far the majority of the descendants of the early Spanish settlers and the original Americans were left with little. The riches of the wealthy landowners grew whilst the bulk of the people were left extremely poor. This uneven distribution of land between the rich and poor settlers and the original Americans unhappily continues today in these now independent countries. The actual social spread was ignored and only the rights of the rich owners of most of the prime land were considered; land often developed by the efforts of others and usually the labors of the original settlers. The real owners of the land, the indigenous population of the Americas were almost completely ignored. Interestingly, and somewhat surprisingly, Portugal itself did not gain full independence until 1910.

This situation was ripe for the birth of freedom fighters, and in 1964, in Colombia; they organized themselves into the *Fuerzas Armadas Revolucionarias de Colombia* (FARC). At first, they were just that – freedom fighters. However, political factions soon became involved inevitably moving them progressively to the left, following Marxist and Leninist thoughts. It wasn't long before these political principles started to dominate all around; with an essentially right-wing government opposing the now left-wing FARC – a civil war was inevitable. Interestingly it was not just between the two main factions of left and right, but also between the numerous private armies that sprang up in support of the coca-growing plantations and later the illegal industries extracting gold.

Colombia is a large country, much of which the government policies pay little attention to. Simply, it is too big to develop a complete infrastructure and consequently too large to supervise. Not surprisingly illicit coca plantations sprang up, as did illegal gold mining.

These illegal groups cleared parts of the forest land for the harvesting of the coca plant. The leaves were then processed on-site, reducing the prepared cocaine to relatively small quantities, which was then easily transportable, even across the often-wild terrain, to the United States. The increasing demand for cocaine, particularly to Europe, was now reflecting in their profits. Unfortunately, these profits did not find their way back to Colombia – they were often invested elsewhere. Money laundering became a major industry, from which many people benefited, possibly more than from the primary drug trade itself. To stop coca production, the government made only token attempts to spray weed killer on the green plantations, and then they only attacked the small farmers who were using coca as their main and sometimes only source of income. From a relatively small acreage of land, they could supply the needs of their families from only small amounts of cocaine. The larger cartel members went unchallenged.

Similarly, with gold, the unlicensed groups treated the land harshly, polluting many of the rivers with mercury used for its extraction and purification. Again, this might have been acceptable if the profits had been returned to Colombia, but no, like the drug money, it was laundered and invested in foreign lands. The basic tragedy was that the development of cocaine and gold benefited only a very few people. Had just part of the money been returned to Colombia there might have been some justification for this illicit trade, and the acceptance of its social evils. It could have been spent on providing reasonable accommodation, education, health facilities and good infrastructure; the whole country would then have benefited and some good would have ensued. The government did little to solve the problem; their only action was improving security rather than helping the people. Fortunately, progress is coming. Medellin, once the main drug city, is redeveloping that part of Colombia to help the poor and the indigenous people, and there are signs once more of community happiness. Medellin is returning to being the *City of Eternal Spring* – famous for its annual flower festival.

Eventually, the infrastructure of Colombia will be developed and then it will be possible to safely grow products from which the country will benefit, such as bananas, cocoa, coffee, and corn. The intrinsic minerals of gold and emeralds will be safely and legally sold to the rest of the world, from which all of us will benefit.

Writing a historical novel presents the author with many challenges. A true historian would chronicle the facts whilst the novelist weaves them, hopefully, into it an interesting and plausible story of people. *The Land of Emeralds* is a story set in recent times, in South and Central America. The author has chosen to center the story on Colombia and the northern parts of South America, Mexico and the Central American countries. It considers the influence the Iberian Peninsula adventurers had on the development of these countries and the economic problems initially beset by the United States of America.

The characters of the novel are developed in the imagination of the author. They are not real people, but the author believes that the basic story could well have reflected the challenges faced by real people, and it could have been a true story about them. Any similarity to actual people is purely by chance.

Cabo San Lucas

'...and I think to myself what a wonderful world,' Louis

Satchmo Armstrong

There is no doubt about it our world is a wonderful place: the trees; the flowers, the lakes and the rivers; the cliffs and the seashore; the mountains, the valleys and the fields. They provide a feast for all our senses, especially our precious eyesight. They also indulge our sense of sound; as we hear the soothing rustle of leaves in a gentle breeze or the babbling of a playful stream, the noisy torrent of a river in flood and the roaring sea as it battles against rocky cliffs. Contrast this to the perfect silence and tranquility of the small hours of the morning or the natural quiet of the mountains and hills away from modern life; it all has to be experienced to be believed. Then, there are the flowers and the trees with their sweet natural fragrances, the source of the perfumes so readily available in modern life. All this comes from nature itself. Even the barren lands have their own sienna tinted beauty. And what about the great mysteries of life itself, the intoxication of pure fresh air and the beauty of the cerulean[1] skies, so splendid they require the ancient language of Latin to describe them, and the many shades of blue reflected in the sky as the direction and intensity of light changes. And why is the sky blue, and why are trees green, and why and who decided the colors of flowers, and the striking pure white of new snowdrops. All these great mysteries originate from one single-source – simply from the sun, the source of all life, in the simple form of light and heat. Scientists would say all-natural life starts from this electromagnetic radiation; traveling over ninety million miles through space before arriving on the surface of the earth. The sun appears to us to have no limits, it has been there since the beginning of time and will no doubt continue to the end of time. Well not quite, scientists also tell us, the sun was made at the time of the Big Bang – 13.8 billion years ago – and from it everything we now know was created. Yes, all of nature was made from the sun. This is truly amazing, almost miraculous. And what about life itself; wildlife, that steadily looks after itself, and last but not least human life, that truly is a miracle. Yes, Satchmo had certainly got it right; the world is a wonderful place, full of beauty and mystery.

I think we all have this view and haven't we all reflected from time to time not only on the beauty of our world but also on its marvels and mysteries. To me, one of its greatest natural features is something we see every day – it is the horizon; something that is real yet it behaves as if it is intangibly imaginary. Whenever I gaze from the shore at the distant

---

[1] Cerulean is from the Latin for sky or heavens, which in turn is from caeruleus, resembling the deep blue of the sky from which the sea receives its color.

horizon of the sea, I am astonished to think I am looking at the only physical straight line that nature gives to us, and, what is more, as we move, this straight natural line is capable of moving mysteriously to different parts of the sky and associated with it there is the strange visual display of the sea always sloping down away from the horizon towards us. Contrast this to the familiar land horizon; it is also just as intangible, it continually moves away as we approach it, we can see it, but cannot reach out to it and touch it, yet we can imagine what might lie beyond. For the sea, we have no such intuitive sense; most of us have no way of telling what is beyond the sea horizon. It could be something quite outside our experience, thoughts, and imagination. Yes, don't we all sometimes stop and contemplate our world and, like Satchmo, don't we all '… think to ourselves what a wonderful world.'

Maybe it was the majesty of the sea, with its mysterious horizon that coaxed our ancestors, especially those on the west of the Iberian Peninsula, to want to give up the security of their homeland and to sail away – away from its plentiful resources and interesting history, out into the unknown. They traveled with their families, on what must frequently have been perilous journeys, to see what was there. Possibly, they were just simply inquisitive, maybe, I don't know. However, once they had made these adventurous voyages to lands, they did not know existed, they were rewarded with a wonderfully rich world, beautiful, and extremely fertile. They very quickly settled and were soon followed by other immigrants to what we now know as the New World. Awaiting them was a treasure trove of opportunities; rewards available to everyone who worked hard. I think that was the real reason they were so adventurous – well, that is what the romantic side of me believes. I don't think it was anything to do with the views that modern historians often proclaim. After all, something must have first driven even the conquistadors to make their not always creditable exploits. And also, I don't think it was anything to do with the possible financial advantage of finding a north-west passage to a shorter silk route to China or a shorter spice route to India. No, I am sure it was simply the desire for a romantic adventure.

I benefited from their inquisitiveness, for it was certainly my adventurous ancestors that brought me to a land where it seems the sun shines incessantly as if it always wants to welcome you. Not only does the sun shine, but the clarity of its light is exceptional. The fact that there are thousands of miles of ocean to the west of the new world, providing pure unpolluted air, is no doubt, the main reason for this clarity. There is certainly something extra special about a south-west aspect; the high-quality light, arriving first from the south and then from the southwest, has something mystical about it – it makes colors deepen until they almost radiate out towards you and everything around seems to have that added sparkle. All this is certainly magnificent and, to me, its gem is Cabo San Lucas, proudly overlooking the Pacific Ocean – the ocean of peace, the blue ocean, the ocean that covers one-third of the planet. Cabo San Lucas is the place I now call home.

My villa enjoys a stunning location, partially hidden from the road. It is just possible to see the outline of what looks to be a typical old Spanish cottage, possibly a relic from the past, yet it is quite new. The architect intended its design to look typically Spanish, fitting comfortably into the beautiful cliff edge vista, and still be light, and airy. His considerable experience of designing such villas was certainly put to the test. Approaching from the road you see a typical white-arched Spanish building that could easily have been several centuries old. The gardens are colorful with beautiful sunny tropical plants. To the left of the villa is a disguised helicopter pad; necessary for my frequent visits to Colombia and the Central Americas. Interestingly, inside the villa there is a sharp architectural time swing; the style is now very different. All the main reception rooms have large picture windows illuminated by the brilliant light of the ocean; they are electrically operated, as also are the blinds. Air conditioning is available, but rarely used since most of the time the patio windows are wide open. All this, together with the open-plan and minimalist décor, gives the impression that the rooms have no walls and that the whole of the villa is floating in the open air. This style and the wonderful climate allow me to take most of my meals outside by the pool, with its marvelous backdrop of the blue ocean.

A large patio surrounds the swimming pool, the shape of which is hard to describe; it is simply a series of connecting sympathetically opposing curves, constructed of blue glazed tiles, attempting to imitate the color of the azure blue sea and sky. Immediately beyond the pool and patio, the gardens, seemingly with no borders, tumble over the edge of the cliff – a kind of Spanish ha-ha. It is a breathtaking example of a modern villa that fits into the authentic rural Mexican landscape.

For me, the bright morning light always prevents further sleep and I find the best thing to do is to get up and, after a glass of ice-cold orange juice, I go down to the beach for a swim in the cool morning water. The sensation is most refreshing and I like nothing better than snorkeling around the rocks by the headland. The colorful tropical fish seem to be iridescent in the crystal-clear water and, to my surprise and interest, they seem to want to scrutinize me just as much as I like to watch them. I would swear that each morning the same fish wait for me to appear and together we greet each other. They seem pleased to see me and together we play. They certainly react to my attempts to touch them, moving to and fro in a happy response. Then, after a while, playtime is over and I bid them farewell and swim back to the beach.

My watch shows it was just 7:05 a.m., and as I stroll along the beach the sun's heat is already starting to burn my skin. This is a routine for me even after the effort of snorkeling for what must have been well over an hour. It is the perfect start to the day. Around the headland, a cruise liner has already anchored and soon excited bronzed holidaymakers will be ferried ashore to enjoy the sights of the beautiful village of Cabo San Lucas, and its magnificent vistas of both land and sea. After traveling to many countries, Cabo San Lucas is still, for me, the world's most idyllic retreat.

Unfortunately, political duties in Bogotá and Cartagena, together with business restraints in the Central Americas and occasionally in the Far East, I am allowed only brief, but mercifully frequent visits to the villa. Then, as the summer heat intensifies, all that changes, and in June and July, I abandon my 'city responsibilities' for two months, to enjoy a quiet way of life. I visit my villa for almost the whole of that uninterrupted period, and I try my very best to live simply. My villa is perched on the most southern tip of the Mexican Baja California peninsula and enjoys the sun from dawn 'till dusk; it is there where for two months of the summer I just sit and think and write. If only those two months were for the whole year, then my life would be perfect.

My housekeeper, Rosa, will not arrive until about nine o'clock, giving me an hour or so to enjoy one of my main passions in life; a pot of the most flavored coffee in the world. My plantation in the Blue Mountains of Jamaica produces the world's best Arabica beans, which are carefully roasted in Kingston and then flown over to me each week. Some say this coffee reminds them of jasmine and peaches and some say wild herbs. For me, it is just wonderfully smooth, aromatic, and tasty. At nine o'clock prompt, Rosa will appear with fresh rolls, and yet a further pot of coffee, and I will breakfast on the terrace by the pool. I allow just thirty minutes each day for the inevitable political and business urgent matters before I settle down to about three hours of writing. To me, I feel I have the peace of a desert island; only occasionally will I see someone, and then they will probably be in one of the small glass-bottomed boats appearing around the headland.

It is not surprising that from time to time I just want to sit and think. After all, I've had a most unusual life and it is both interesting and revealing to think about it. My early life was spent in a seminary where I would have stayed had it not been for the drug barons of South America. It was also because of these drug barons that I inadvertently became a drug peddler to provide an income for my family, and as a consequence, ended up serving a prison sentence in England. After that, I made sure my life was uncomplicatedly simple. I worked at my small market stall on the beach, selling jewelry. Then, after making an unusual acquaintance with a millionaire couple from Los Angeles, my life changed as I also did my beach marketing business. Quickly, it developed into a very large and extensive retail company still based essentially on beach marketing, but now selling emeralds from Colombia uniquely designed by my sister Maria. At first, it had been relatively low-cost jewelry made from emerald chips; later it moved into very expensive emerald jewelry, often specially made to customer requirements. It was not long before I started to work in other commercial areas, particularly coffee, keeping well away from my brief unfortunate connection with the drug business. The expansion of my coffee plantation and emerald marketing businesses was extremely challenging, and both were complicated by having to deal with the ever-controlling cartels of Central America. After my success, particularly, against these various coffee cartels in Costa Rica and Colombia, it was inevitable that I found myself being persuaded to take part in political activities – something I initially had no wish to do.

I am now a very wealthy man and I have been able to buy a very modern and beautiful villa right on the edge of the cliffs at Cabo San Lucas, overlooking the ever azure blue sea. Despite my wealth and the extravagance of my villa, where I spend as much time as possible, my life is very simple. And this inevitably makes me think about the complications of life in Central America and somewhat strangely gives me time for my hobby of writing novels, essentially romantic stories. They have no connection whatsoever to do with my past. It is simply something that I like to do. For the last few years, I have written two novels each summer and I am just finishing my eighth. Mornings in Cabo San Lucas are just perfect. I live alone, and my mornings follow the same set pattern that rarely changes. I normally meet only three people all day – Rosa, my housekeeper, José, her husband, and my gardener, and Sylvia, my secretary.

In about three hours, I will give Silvia about five thousand handwritten words to type. She will then take them away and type them. Next day, we will go through the manuscript and discuss possible alterations. I very much value her advice and criticism, even though I don't always want to take it. Writing, like many creative arts, is much more perspiration than inspiration; in my case, it is more than ninety percent of my total effort. After my first novel, my writing income soared. Not that I needed the money – I was already very wealthy with more money than I could ever spend or want to spend. I simply find writing a very pleasant and beautiful creative way of using my leisure time. It continuously presents me with a challenge; there is always a new experience to investigate and, above all, it gives me a chance to think – one of the most rewarding of all human endeavors. All my life I have been a thinker; especially in my youth days and when I was in prison – where I had ample opportunity to make it almost a perfect art.

Just after lunch, Sylvia will arrive, usually around 2 p.m. Today she was a little earlier; as her small daughter, Anna, was to go to friends for tea, and Sylvia wanted to be home by about 3.30 in time to take her. Before we started work, we chatted for a while as we often did. Sylvia started by saying, 'Now that your latest novel is almost complete, why don't you write about your own life. After all, it has been just as exciting, if not more so than the imaginary lives of the characters you write about in your novels.'

What a strange coincidence, for she had said exactly what I had been thinking only this very morning whilst snorkeling in the crystal-clear water near the rocks; I had mused a little to myself on making my own life the story for a novel. Not an autobiography, for that is only for well-known and famous people, but a story based on some of the events of my own life, it might just be interesting.

The Night of the Iguana and Playa

Mismaloya

I was in my early twenties when I saw the film *The Night of the Iguana*. The whole of Acapulco was abuzz with the romance of Elizabeth Taylor and Richard Burton. Consequently, this underdeveloped part of the Pacific coast of Mexico become very much the in-place for the 'Californian set'. I could see this from the sales at my little market stall in the old part of the city. In 1963, the filming of the *Night of the Iguana* opened the door to prosperity and fame for Puerto Vallarta and the whole of the Mexican Pacific coast. Elizabeth Taylor and Richard Burton both bought houses in the old town; in fact, they had them connected by a bridge. Deborah Kerr, Ava Gardner, Sue Lyon, and Richard Burton were all part of John Houston's famous cast list, and scenes of the film were being shot at Playa Mismaloya. It was, therefore, not surprising that there was so much interest. For me the film was only moderately interesting; although perhaps any film based on a play by Tennessee Williams and directed by John Houston, with such a glamorous cast, was bound to be successful and certainly would bring immediate fame to this little-known western coast of Mexico. Not surprisingly, American and Mexican entrepreneurs were quick to take advantage. The Diamante part of the Acapulco region, in the direction of Caleta, was no longer to be the poor part of Acapulco; now it was the *New Acapulco*, with luxury hotels, expensive apartments, and all the associated trappings of elegant shops together with the inevitable extravagant boutiques. It was, I suppose, just the place for my first real experience of true commercial entrepreneurial creativity.

I was certainly benefiting from the jewelry I sold to the American tourists; jewelry made from emeralds mined in the hills of Colombia and cut in the workshops of Cartagena. They were very popular with the tourists, and as more and more Americans visited Acapulco my income increased, and so did my desire to have the independence that this wealth could bring me.

Market stallholders meet a wide range of customers and it was from a meeting with one particular gentleman and his wife that I was invited to see one of the first showings of this famous film with its distinguished cast. I was fluent in Spanish, of course, nearly so in French and German, and pretty fluent in English, and it was this, I think, that made this wealthy couple from Los Angeles befriend me. At first, they were impressed by the fact that a market stallholder appeared to be so well educated. Mrs. Bunny Golding had purchased a necklace of Colombian square-cut emeralds from me, and she and her husband were impressed by my description of where the stones had been mined, and how they had been designed, cut and set. They were also impressed with my language skills. Although they were very familiar with Acapulco, and had frequently visited many of its attractions, its hotels and nightclubs, it was clear to me that they knew very little about real Mexico.

Big Daddy and Bunny frequently passed my beach stall and would often stop for a chat. One afternoon, they invited me to join them for dinner at one of the many small beach tavernas. For me, the evening was just perfect and the food delicious. As we chatted it transpired that Big Daddy, as I suspected, would like to know more about real Mexico, its people, and their lifestyles. The more I told them the more they wanted to know, and this swelled their interest so much that they engaged me as their guide. They were interested in the real Mexico and were anxious to experience its true ambiance and its food, not just the atmosphere prepared for tourists, and certainly not canned Tijuana music. I could offer them something much more authentically Mexican. I had friends who had a traditional restaurant at their hacienda in the mountains; I was pretty sure they could provide an evening experience to remember and at Big Daddy's request, I made the arrangements.

The Golding's were very much intrigued by the Elizabeth Taylor-Richard Burton affair as were all Americans, and being influential people, they were given the opportunity, whilst they were still in Mexico, to see an early private viewing of this much talked about the film. It was my good fortune to be asked to join them. I thought it would be an interesting film, but I didn't think it was about real Mexico – actually it was a pleasant story with a famous cast list.

The day after seeing the film, we decided to go to my friends' hacienda. I arrived at the Las Brisas Hotel in the late afternoon in a Hertz limousine hire car. The plan was to take them into the mountains behind the hills to a small rural

Mexican restaurant. There we would dine in an authentic style and listen to live Tijuana music, whilst watching the sunset over the Pacific Ocean. At the insistence of Big Daddy, I had on board a crate of high quality pure bottled water, and a mobile refrigerator full of crushed ice made from that same water. Bunny and Big Daddy, having previously had bitter experiences of Mexican bar cocktails, did not want to take any chances.

The late afternoon sun was still very hot and Bunny decided to first take a swim at the beach club before embarking on the evening's activities in what would then be in the cooler mountain air. This sounded perfect to me, and it would be my first experience of such luxury. The pool looked inviting, located in magnificent surroundings, adorned with bougainvillea, hibiscus, oleander, and morning glory – all delightfully fragrant in their colorful array. The huge irregular amoeba-shaped pool, with small geisha-like bridges at each isthmus, looked stunningly attractive. All were shaded by palm trees, and surrounded with strategically submerged barstools; the azure blue water was certainly most inviting. We changed and entered the pool. Initially, this was an uncomfortable experience; the heat of the mid-day sun had made walking with bare feet on the delicately colored mosaic tiles quite painful. Fortunately, once we were in the pool the caressing water relieved all sensations of burning and for almost an hour, we experienced the most wonderful sensations – sensations new to me. Of course, I had often swum in the beautiful waters of the Pacific Ocean, but to swim in such wonderful surroundings, and to experience the life of a millionaire, if only for a few hours, was truly outstanding – it was divine.

For a while, we lounged in the sun to fully dry our bodies, and acclimatize ourselves to the evening air, then we set off, at about 6:30 pm, for the mountain hacienda. Little formality was expected, and it took Bunny only a few minutes to dress.

Driving through the outskirts of Acapulco is itself an interesting experience, initially passing the expensive hotels and villas that decorate and dominate the region; each trying to outdo its neighbor in architectural style, size and natural pascal colors. Then the whole atmosphere slowly starts to change as does the very well maintained and clean roads; gradually the wonderful houses are returning to their Spanish origins – typical Spanish dwellings whose original roots, no doubt, dated back to the first years of Spanish occupation. For me, they showed old Acapulco with its past charms and natural quaintness; I am not at all certain whether I like the artificial nature of many of the expensive millionaire's villas and hotels. For decades, these cottages have enjoyed and sometimes endured the western sun, with only the minimum of maintenance. They have basked in the warm atmosphere of the Pacific Ocean air and have been adorned with an ever-present array of beautiful shrubs and trees – they are simply charming. At first, the mountain road was very good; then after a few miles, it started to deteriorate slowly at first then more rapidly, to what was now little more than a track. Once it had been a metalized road, but after years of neglect, the surface was now full of potholes, the areas of which were sometimes almost greater than parts of the true surface. I now had to drive very slowly, sometimes stopping and reversing to negotiate a suitable path between the often too deep to drive through holes.

Forty-five minutes later, Philippe Gonzales and his wife,

Loreto, greeted us. I had telephoned earlier to warn them that tonight they would be host to an interesting wealthy couple from Los Angeles who wished to sample their true Mexican hospitality.

Sipping ice-cold margaritas and nibbled delicious tortillas dipped in home-made salsa, we chatted. Bunny was inquisitive about all things Mexican and we chatted for nearly an hour with Philippe and Loreto, who were equally interested in American life, and the world of Los Angeles. Eventually, the conversation moved to me and how I came to speak English so well, and yet only work at a market stall. At first, I was very guarded in what I said; then as the tequila took over, and with the evocative Tijuana music in my ears, I started to tell them my story.

Cartagena

I was fortunate to be born in the beautiful country of Colombia, the eldest of a large family living on the edge of Cartagena. The beautiful city of Cartagena, set on the magnificent Caribbean Sea, was one of the first Spanish settlements in Central and South America – the main colonization taking place between the sixteenth and eighteenth centuries. Not surprisingly, during that early period, there was a real variability of success between the many groups of arriving settlers; some became rich whilst others were less fortunate. The early settlers had the opportunity to select the best and most fertile land – they selected good accessible land, close to the shore, and easy to cultivate, whilst the later settlers were not so fortunate and many of them ended up working for the descendants of the now rich early immigrants. It was inevitable that all did not benefit equally from for their hard work; fortune often had very different effects on each of them, and so it was in all the Americas. What happened in the early days had a big influence on the development of the New World, both during and after the Spanish occupation. As so often happens it was the rich who benefited, often at the expense of the poor.

My family had been fortunate, but was in no way rich, we were very close and content. When I was eight years old, the parish priest Dom Juan Ignacio, started to teach me Latin. He had been impressed at the speed with which I mastered the Latin Mass responses and correctly detected that I had a flair for languages. It was then only a short step for me to be admitted to the Catholic seminary in the hills above Cartagena, about twenty kilometers outside the city. My parents were only too pleased to let the church take over my education and being good Catholics, a priest in the family was undoubtedly something to be proud of.

I must say, life in the seminary was good; it was interesting, stimulating and challenging. The other students were extremely friendly and together we all had both interesting and happy times. Being relatively near home, I would frequently see my parents and brothers and sisters – they enjoyed a day out in the hills in the peace and tranquility of the seminary. Life progressed in a very orderly and agreeable manner. We would rise early in the morning and go to the chapel for the principal Mass of the day; frequently we would assist the many priests with their individual Masses. This was before Vatican II and concelebrating Mass was rare, indeed if it happened at all. Recreation played an important part in our lives, with football dominating. It was an idyllic time and I made friendships that were to last for the rest of my life.

Time passed peacefully and soon I was eighteen; for ten years I had enjoyed the tranquil life of a seminarian, now it was time to commence theology and philosophy studies. They would last for six years before my ordination – then, quite out of the blue, my life dramatically changed. My father was suddenly taken ill and, after a short illness, sadly died. My mother was left with four young children to look after with no regular income. She might have just been able to manage, but it would have been a great strain; I felt I had no option but to leave the seminary, for a while at least, and try to secure a regular income so that I could help – perhaps for a year or so. We would then have some money and at the same time, I could help her look after my brothers and sisters. I could return to the seminary later.

Getting a job was easier said than done. There were very few jobs available. I was hardly the type to do manual work, although I certainly would have considered it. Then, to my surprise, I was approached by an old school friend. He remembered that I was very good at Latin and quite good at English. He introduced me to an international courier company who was recruiting agents to act for them, making journeys between South America and Europe. With my knowledge of Spanish and some English and with a background of reliability, having been a seminarian, I was given a trial to carry small packages of valuable emeralds to Paris, Frankfurt, and London. It was a pleasant well-paid job and I received $50 per trip, and I could sometimes make three trips a week. To me, that was a large amount of money. All I had to do was collect a parcel from the courier company in Cartagena and deliver it to the country involved. They provided me with air tickets and hotel accommodation. After a while, I was asked to transport other small packages, and for that, I was paid considerably more – $300 per trip. It was then that I began to think I might be involved in something more sinister and possibly even illegal. The packages were small and sealed; I did not know what they contained – was it perhaps cocaine? I knew pure cocaine was likely to be in small quantities.

Now with an income of over a thousand US dollars per week, all my family's financial problems were completely solved. But should I be making these journeys? My justification was that I did not know what the packages contained – I only had suspicions – I did not know. What I knew was that I was now able to feed and clothe all my immediate family and also provide for their education. There was even sufficient money available to help them start businesses that would give them future personal financial security.

What should I do? Without realizing it, I was now in a very difficult position – probably engaging in drug trafficking from South America to Europe. Instinctively, I was concerned and certainly did not want to be involved in an industry that I knew very little about, except that it was evil, or at least there was a fundamental evil aspect to it. I knew I should not be involved in anything like this, especially after only just leaving the seminary. Quite simply, I should not be involved in any illegal transactions. I knew very little about the drug trade other than that it existed and that in one way or another it caused serious problems, particularly to those who became addicted to them.

I had my suspicions as soon as my pay per journey dramatically increased, and I felt then that inevitably problems would follow. I was caught up in a dilemma of either saying no or continuing to provide for the whole of my family. Under the circumstances, I felt I had no option but to continue. I tried to justify it by thinking that there are two sides to the drug industry and users must take equal responsibility – without users, there would be no trade. Then, to my dismay, one of the

South American drug cartels decided to take over the extensive land of my old seminary. Mainly, they were after the agricultural land, but they were also happy to close the seminary down. The church had always been a nuisance to them actively fighting their exploitation of people, especially those unable to help themselves.

The cartel wanted more drugs, and they wanted drugs that were easily produced; for this, good soil, good access and a plentiful supply of laborers were required. Previously, clandestine growing deep in the forest had its advantages – they were largely unseen and unknown. Now, they didn't seem to be concerned about that. The area around the seminary was just right and that was all that dominated their thinking. They had wanted it for some time, but it was not for sale and certainly not to the drug industry. Persuasion did not help so the cartel simply took the land, with officialdom turning a blind eye; probably they were part of the cartel or at least recipients of their bribes.

It would appear the drug cartels, certainly in Central and South America, had never had it so good. You might have thought that was enough for them. No, they were quite certain that there was more profit for the taking. Initially, the US was the main area for them. Europe was hardly involved; it was just waiting there to be tapped. Quite simply, there was much more money to be made, money for all, even after paying the necessary bribery fees there was still plenty left. Perhaps it was not surprising that all involved wanted more, particularly when they saw it was possible. When greed is around it has no limits and, usually, it is there to stay.

It wasn't long before the drug cartels realized I had linguistic skills, and that they could be very useful. They were now actively looking for more couriers to deliver drugs to all the countries of Europe, in particular to England, Germany, Italy, France and Spain. They were prepared to pay considerable amounts of money to access these cities and I was asked if I would make a list of all the different ways a courier could enter them. I was asked to find as many cities as possible that could be visited sequentially so that, at least in the first instance, the suspicion that a courier was making numerous visits would not be aroused. The plan was for me and others to make numerous journeys to different parts of Europe such that effectively it would look, at least at first glance, as if only single journeys were being made by private citizens. Essentially, we would make one visit per courier per city. Hopefully, to the local customs officials, it would look as if it was only an occasional non-routine visit. My task was to compile a list of as many places as possible that could be innocently visited in this way. A courier could then make journeys to different European cities using various methods of entry, such that suspicion was avoided. With the aid of airline schedules and timetables for trains and ferries, I was surprised how many separate unrelated journeys from South America to Europe could be made in a single week, possibly staying for one or two nights in a single location. I found it was relatively easy to make five visits per week and occasionally I managed to make more than one in a single day. However, there was one major problem and that was the number of passport stamps that were accumulating on my passport. The cartels were most impressed with my preliminary work and to them, the passport problem was easily solved. Their tentacles spread extensively and they could readily provide me with frequent replacement passports. I only had to ask and they would provide me with another passport accurately dated and suitably artificially aged so that only very careful examination would reveal it was forged. I was now in a position to make numerous journeys to Europe, and what is more, I was able to plan a system for others to make similar journeys. Effectively, I was the control and system organizer for shipping drugs from South America to Europe. As the process developed, I started to carry not only small parcels but also additional parcels. Sometimes, I would take with me what looked like an innocuously large tube of toothpaste – one I was using – and inside it was a capsule full of one of the more expensive drugs. Cannabis and cocaine were carried in the sides of my hold-all, which was treated to disguise any tell tail smells detectible by sniffer dogs. All I had to do was make the appropriate travel arrangements and enjoy the journey. I was following a prearranged system of giving my drugs to a fence in the city I visited. I did not even have to plan for the handover. I would be contacted at my hotel often only a few minutes after arrival. The handover would then take place and sometimes, not always, I received money to take back home.

Handling money was itself now becoming a problem. Of course, currencies such as the British pound or any of the European currencies and the American dollar are extremely useful in world trade; however, there was still a distinct problem of carrying excessive amounts of loose money possibly giving the suspicion of illegal activity. How could someone from South America have so much money, actually in cash? It certainly might indicate that I was involved in something like the drug trade, or perhaps its associated money laundering. I had to avoid this at all costs. What could I do? Many of the South American currencies are restricted currencies with very few people trading in them; they were not often involved in international banking. The severe restrictions on the amount of money a foreign company trading with South American countries could handle, caused additional problems. I wasn't certain what I should do; the cartel could not help, so I must solve the problem myself. I was getting close to a state of sheer exasperation – I had to find a solution. How to deal with it was a real headache, and then by chance, I found myself outside the Soviet Embassy in London and it occurred to me perhaps it was here I could find a solution. After all, they wanted western currency. The Soviets are a law unto themselves and I knew that they were becoming more and more involved in Central and South America, hoping to spread their political influence to regions close to the United States – possibly they could help. Plucking up courage, I went inside and asked if I could discuss my predicament with them. Were they in a position to provide me with some kind of financial arrangement; one that would help both of us? As I expected, they were extremely pleased to get hold of hard European currency and we soon found a way of solving my problem. I was to convert all my currency into Soviet rubles whilst in Europe, and when back in South America I would visit the Soviet Embassy and they would provide me with banking facilities so that I could convert this money gradually into local currencies. For this, I was paid US $200 per trip, about $30,000 each month. To me, this was an immense amount of money. I now had enough money to provide for my family. I was not at all happy with what I was doing, but it was the only way I could earn that kind of money. After my fees, the remainder was returned to various banking accounts belonging to the cartel.

I was a member of a large family and they were all benefiting. Together they were able to absorb much of the money into their lives without appearing as if they had suddenly become unaccountably wealthy. Colombia was now at the stage of becoming domestically modernized and I asked all my family, where possible, to buy capital goods with some of the money. By this process, we managed to convert all my European money into pesos without there being any direct connection with a money-laundering route and certainly not one that could easily be investigated. It would be, of course, very difficult to investigate what was happening behind the closed doors of the Soviet Union Embassy. My approach to money laundering met with considerable approval by the members of the cartel. It was one of their major problems – how to move large amounts of money in such a way that its history was destroyed or at least disguised. Money laundering has always been a problem for the drug trade; it is not easy to find a way to convert money into non-traceable cash or assets. To use the Soviet Union was a way that had not occurred to the cartels; now they were giving instructions to all their couriers to follow a similar route, if possible. They were so pleased with my efforts they rewarded me with a magnificently square cut emerald ring worth about $40,000; it just shows how much money was being made that they were prepared to reward those who helped them in such a way. I still have this magnificent emerald ring with its beautiful stone – it is worth much more than any diamond of similar size.

Involuntarily, I had become involved in the drug trade. I did it simply for the money; there was no work in Cartagena and with the South American drug cartels running the countryside it was the only possible way for me to earn money;

I had become part of one of the cartels. At eighteen years I knew this trade had many evil aspects. However, living in a poor country where near starving is almost routine and where medical assistance is virtually unavailable, the often-caring aspects of the cartels overruled any moral issues. After all, South America was getting the benefits from the drugs and little of the disadvantages. It was the rich, developed countries such as the USA and now Europe, that had to cope with all its social consequences and its evils.

Successive government administrations had sought to stop its spread by the simple expedient of making it a criminal activity – a process that has to this day failed. The fact is that whilst there are users there will always be growers and sellers, and someone, somewhere, will always find a way to grow, process, and distribute cannabis, cocaine, and heroin.

England

It was not surprising that after eighteen months of almost daily traveling to different capitals in Europe, I was arrested flying into Heathrow. I was on an Air France flight from Paris, and I was carrying four kilograms of cocaine. What happened then was legally interesting and, to some extent, helpful to me. This was because at that time I was one of the first people to be found carrying significant amounts of illegal drugs into Britain and I had arrived on a flight I boarded in Paris, not in Colombia.

After searching my person and my luggage and also after some initial interrogation, I was placed in police custody. I had only been there for a few hours when I was introduced to Fr. John, the Catholic chaplain. The arresting officers, realizing I was from Colombia, thought I was probably a Catholic and they sent for him, hoping that he could help with the inevitable language problems. As a Catholic priest, Fr. John was immediately interested in me and my predicament. He knew very little Spanish, and to help we spoke in Latin. Not only did our conversation suddenly become easy, but more than that it indicated to him I was or had been a seminarian; only such people were likely to be able to converse with such fluency in an ancient language – he was now even more intrigued. Fr. John knew little of life in Colombia, although he had once visited a school in El Salvador. It concerned him very much to think my seminarian life had so abruptly come to an end. To him, that was more important than my new life with the drug cartel. I told him it was only a temporary pause and somewhat unconvincingly I think he accepted it. Fr. John was a constant visitor and was instrumental in helping me get assistance and facilities whilst held in detention.

It was the time when liberation theology was beginning to take place in South America, and many of the European clergies were very interested in what was happening. The Vatican itself was concerned that priests were actively taking part in lay activities and politics, and that there might even be the possibility of them becoming a little too left-wing – or rather that they may be accused of being left-wing. So much so, that the Pope had made several visits to some of the South American countries; he was afraid that something was happening that might get out of control. Fr. John was very interested in all this and he questioned me in great detail as to what was happening and the extent to which liberation theology was affecting people and the church and how the local and national politicians were dealing with it. We would spend long sessions discussing it.

Liberation theology – the unusual mixture of left-wing socialist theory and Christian principles – was causing the church to wonder precisely what was going on. The Vatican expressed its concerns to the South American bishops and both Pope Paul VI and Pope John Paul II made visits to discuss with the local bishops what was happening. The current challenging economic and welfare problems, and the effect it was having on the poor people under their charge; had made it necessary for the local church to intervene – the Vatican's main fear was there were many fundamental dangers attached to a mixture of Marxism and Christianity. It has always been the view that the church should steer away from political involvement and when priests started to become practically involved in what was happening there was cause for concern.

There should be no need for the church to be involved in state affairs. With good political organization the poor of South America should be adequately catered for, and poverty should not exist.

It had been inevitable, as the development of the Americas took place, that the settlers had mixed success; some did extremely well and others not so well. Over the years, the difference between these various groups widened. When decolonization took place, this uneven distribution was cemented into territorial land allocations; thus, having the inescapable result that a relatively small number of people became extremely rich whilst most remained poor. The Latin American countries are now all independent, but the distribution of wealth in Central America has not changed. Most people are poor and a small number are very rich. It is, therefore, not surprising that the Catholic Church became involved and liberation theology was conceived; the ground was fertile and ready for these new thoughts to germinate and grow. Back in Europe, the thoughts of Karl Marx were well known, and a mixture of Christianity and Marxism seemed to be a very unnatural mix. This might not have been so had Marx not been so openly atheistic, preaching the view that many of the poor people of the world only followed religious beliefs for consolation. Marx was well known for saying, 'religion that was the opium of the poor'. That was all well and good, but the principle of Karl Marx that each person should do his best and in return his needs should be catered for should not have ventured into religious affairs.

Karl Marx's views have some conceptual merit; however, in reality, a very different situation occurs. Some people work much harder than others and some are blessed with good fortune and good health; all this means a difference or gap starts to develop between people – some of them can contribute much more than their needs whilst others cannot. This then itself leads to the very basis of capitalism and from it a market economy. Had this difference not been allowed to occur, then modern countries would not have developed and as a consequence, we would not have gained the rewards we have in present life – this would have been to the detriment of all. A politically well-developed country should be able to provide good and adequate work for everybody. When this is not done, there is inevitably political concern and inequality is often founded on individual greed. It was not surprising that someone had to look after the poor people and so often this was left to religious organizations – it was from this that the seeds of liberation theology were sown.

There is now the possibility of a very potentially serious situation occurring in Central America. If Marxism and then communism were to develop close to the United States, there would inevitably be severe consequences. This certainly was of great concern in the United States and equally of concern to the Vatican, especially when priests were becoming more and more politically active – a task they were not by any means trained for. The church had always wanted to keep away from purely political matters; it regarded itself as having sufficient work in looking after the spiritual welfare of people. Pope Paul VI and Pope John Paul II visited Central and South America on several occasions, attempting to guide its priests to a situation that did not involve itself with political conquest. Pope Benedict XVI and Pope Francis followed similarly, especially in the days before they were made Popes.

Fr. John was interested in liberation theology, but he was much more interested in trying to make sure that I continued my studies in theology and philosophy. However, today I was keener on taking advantage of the possible opportunity for study, particularly languages.

The lawyers involved in my case were trying to bring about a solution. The Colombian officials were none too happy with both the French and the British, who were claiming that the root problem of my drug trafficking activities originated in Colombia, and that they were the country responsible for what was happening. Colombia was not prepared to accept the responsibility for what they believed was a problem caused by people in Britain and all the other countries who wished to buy illicitly available drugs. A legal battle ensued as to whether I should be dealt with by British or French law; because Colombia had no jurisdiction in Britain its views were hardly considered. Needless to say, the Colombian government was unhappy with what was happening and spent a considerable amount of time and effort on my case. No way did they want the rest of the world to think that they were one of the principal suppliers of drugs to the civilized countries of North America and Europe; the responsibility rested elsewhere. The net effect of all this international debate and confusion was that I was kept on remand in England for a very long time, whilst the

English, French and Colombian lawyers argued where the responsibility for my case lay. There was certainly a real lack of inter-country cooperation between them.

Marooned in England in a relatively pleasant remand center with very little to do and still young and active, I decided the best thing was to make use of my time by studying. Fr. John was now playing a big part in helping me further my interest in foreign languages; realizing that whilst I was in England I had the opportunity perfect my English. I now had the chance to try and get it up to a high standard. It is a feature of British law that until you are found guilty you must stay in a special detention center on remand. This is similar to a prison, but much more pleasant, giving the inmates considerable freedom. I was encouraged to make good use of my time and consequently they were only too pleased to provide me with private tuition in English. Fr. John was also willing to help and it wasn't long before I was speaking English to a very high standard; it no longer had the hesitance of a foreign tourist. My desire to make the most of my opportunities quickly extended my linguistic skills to French and German, again with the aid of private tuition. To help with these studies, I was permitted to have a small portable radio in my room; this allowed my language studies to progress rapidly. The radio had a short-wave channel so I could listen to English, French, German and Spanish programs. Also, since I was on remand, I was allowed Colombian Embassy access, and they were eager to provide me with newspapers, magazines and books in all of these languages. With Fr. John's assistance and that of his chaplaincy colleagues, my theology and physiology studies were also continuing.

Eventually, the fact that I had been bringing drugs into England dominated the legal argument, and I was tried and sentenced at the Old Bailey to ten years imprisonment, to be served in England.

My first parole was after only one third into the sentence, and I was told by the Home Office that I was to be released and that I would immediately be deported to Colombia. Rather interestingly, I had been on remand for such a long time that I had spent only a few months actually in prison.

I wasn't at all certain whether being sent back to Colombia was in my best interest and I questioned it, but my plea not to be sent back to Cartagena went unheeded. I wondered if the cartel might be unhappy with one of their couriers being caught, especially since I was being released after only one-third of a ten-year sentence, it might suggest to them my complicity. Fortunately, they were more realistic than this, recognizing that capture was inevitable, and they accepted that I had been more than helpful to them. In fact, throughout my imprisonment, they had been looking after my family.

Panama City

Early on the 1st of May, I was taken to Heathrow and put on board BA 197, British Airways 10.55 daily flight to Cartagena. I was now nearly twenty-one years old. The frills of my earlier transatlantic flights that had led to my incarceration were still in my mind, and I looked forward to twelve hours of eating and drinking in the luxury of a modern airliner. That's how it is on a modern transatlantic journey; there is little passenger activity onboard and they rarely move from their seats. They just eat, drink, read, and sleep.

Then, it was as if my prayers had been answered, and with little less than ninety minutes before touchdown the captain announced that a severe electric storm over the southern Caribbean Sea would mean that we would be landing in Panama City. A flight for me to Cartagena would be available in due course; the British Airways flight itself was to fly north to San Diego. I pondered where I wanted to go! Once on the ground, I knew I would be free from British Authorities jurisdiction and that was something, I did not want to go back to Cartagena – at least not immediately. Realistically, nowhere else was likely to want me. I was, therefore, a free man; that is, as free as a man could be with no money and no job. My first night in Panama City was spent with the Colombian Fathers; sadly, it could be only for one night. They were unable to help me any longer, not wanting to be connected with an ex-fugitive.

The next day, I set off to find a job. Quite a task; for in Panama City there is insufficient work for their own people let alone for other nationals. In any event, I did not have a work permit, only an out-of-date Colombian passport. My first job was to visit the embassy and get my papers renewed. Fearing that I had stolen my old passport, they would not replace it with a new one, nor would they return the old one until further investigations concerning my identity had first been carried out. Effectively, I was now marooned in Panama City without a job, and without papers that would allow me to enter another country

For three months I lived on the streets or in the hills. Occasionally I would receive temporary employment carrying out manual work on a farm or at a villa. Then luck came my way. I came across a new villa having its garden landscaped. The terrain was steep and wild and machines could not get near to it so all the work had to be carried out manually. At first, I received only food and a tent to live in as payment. Later, as the work progressed, the villa owner was so pleased with my efforts he insisted that the contractor start to pay me a regular wage. It wasn't very much, but it was money – the first I had earned since arriving in Panama five months earlier.

One day, whilst I was working on a very difficult part of the garden, the young mistress of the house, Mrs. Lopez, spoke to me. She was American, not much older than me, and was pleased to find one of the contractors who spoke English; her Spanish was insufficient to explain exactly how she wished them to landscape this difficult terrain. I then started to become her interpreter on her frequent visits to the villa. My luck then ran out and sadly, after six weeks, I was notified by the authorities that I could not continue working without a permit and must reapply to the appropriate government department. My heart sank; I had been beginning to enjoy the first success of working for my independence and now I knew I would likely be out of work again. More than that, I was concerned about the ever-present possibility of deportation, but to where having no papers I was effectively stateless.

Mrs. Lopez noticed I was rather preoccupied and eventually persuaded me to tell her why. Her response was dramatic; she was a lady who knew what she wanted and moved quickly to get it. Very soon, her husband's lawyer arrived on the site charged with the task of getting me identity papers and a work permit.

Whilst I talked, Mrs. Lopez listened. The lawyer went through the whole of my life. I could see her eyes widen at some of the detail. I told him how the cartel had changed my life from being a seminarian to becoming a convicted criminal in a foreign land and now a stateless person whom bureaucracy did not want to own.

Mr. Salcedo listened intently and wrote copious notes. After about two hours, he shook his head.

'This is the most difficult and most unusual case I have ever had to handle. I'm far from sure what I can do; I'm not even certain how to begin.'

'It's straightforward,' interrupted Mrs. Lopez. 'If I promise Feliciano work as my assistant then you can get him Panamanian papers.'

'But, Mrs. Lopez, you can only give him work if he has

special talents not regularly found in Panama.'

'He has special talents. He speaks fluent English, German and French as well as his native Spanish. My husband and I only speak English and we are often at a complete loss,' was her reply.

Shaking his head, he muttered, 'I will try, but I'm far from hopeful.' With that, he and Mrs. Lopez parted.

For two weeks I heard nothing. Then a very excited Mrs. Lopez invited me to the poolside to talk. 'I have just received this letter from Mr. Salcedo,' she exclaimed. 'You must visit the Department of the Interior with him and then, if they are happy and convinced with what Mr. Salcedo has said to them, on your behalf, they will grant you a work permit and later citizenship,' she smiled. 'You are effectively being put on probation.'

Mrs. Lopez looked stunningly beautiful. She had just finished breakfast and yet she was dressed for the day. She wore a pure white mini-skirted dress and white open sandals. As we sat facing each other, a gentle breeze repeatedly lifted the delicate material of her skirt revealing her long sun-tanned legs. Either she did not notice this was happening or she was happy to allow me to see her legs. She looked lovely.

I was uncertain what assistant meant and at first, I was a little apprehensive. I realized that she was a very pleasant and lovely lady; although I did begin to wonder. I need not have done, for she always behaved impeccably. At about twenty-three years, she realized she was still attractive and liked men to admire her – that was all. Many times, I saw her beautiful silhouette, but this was always natural – it was simply the clothes she was wearing and the tantalizing breezes around the villa. We did not have an affair; I simply was her Central

American confident. Her husband was happy to see me around and I helped them both deal with the local bureaucracy, on matters, not requiring the legal representation of Mr. Salcedo. After a while, she showed an interest in learning Spanish and asked if I could help her. I started giving her lessons daily; sometimes her husband would join us. She was a natural and took to learning very easily. He was not really interested and very soon dropped behind. I very much enjoyed joining her around the pool where we would together work out the Spanish that would be of real use to her. This caused me some problems with my colleagues when they realized I was being treated specially, and I suppose naturally they thought there may be an ulterior motive – that was not case. Everything was proper as I would have expected – Mrs. Lopez was a lady. Life progressed in an extremely pleasant way for me. I tried hard to make sure that my colleagues received plenty of effort from me, and I was always delighted when I was called to the poolside for what was our daily Spanish lesson.

Life to me was ideal. Then suddenly, after about three years, she had to return to the US for reasons she did not reveal. She wanted me to go with her, but her attempts to bring this about were in vain. My previous connection with the drug trade was so important to the US authorities that even her powerful influence was ineffective.

On the morning she left, she had real tears in her eyes as she kissed me goodbye. No promises were made to meet again; we both knew that would be unlikely. For a moment, she held her body very close to me, and then, with a wave and a big smile, she dashed to the car and was gone. I watched as it disappeared down the lane — she did not turn back. Would I ever see or hear from her again?

Back in Cartagena

I lived alone in Mrs. Lopez's villa for nearly eight months. Then on Tuesday, 5 June, Mr. Salcedo arrived to tell me that the villa had now been sold. He gave me a letter from the Bank of Panama showing I now had a new account containing $50,000, a present from Mrs. Lopez. This, together with the money I still had in Colombia, assuming I could get hold of it, and my emerald ring, made me rich by Central American standards, but still, I was homeless. Perhaps now I should return to Cartagena!

Bunny was listening intently. My life story was now almost up-to-date, for it was shortly after that I returned home to Cartagena and moved, by chance, into emerald trade.

I walked nervously past the immigration officials at Cartagena airport. With only a glance at my passport and a flurry of their ink date stamp, I was soon out on the streets. Marcia, my younger sister, was there to meet me; if it had not been for a recent photograph, I would not have recognized her. I had not seen her for nearly seven years. Last time I saw her she was only sixteen years old now she was fully grown and beautiful.

'Feliciano,' she cried out. 'Feliciano.'

For many minutes, we hugged and kissed. She then turned and waved and a few minutes later a taxi appeared with her husband, Eugene, at the wheel. Along the roads, we traveled until we were almost in the hills; turning left we entered a small plantation, the end of which was our family hacienda. I was home.

My mother was well and the hacienda had hardly changed, only Marcia, Eugene and their children lived with her. But today the house was full of all my brothers and sisters; they had all arrived to greet me. The celebrations went on long into the night. An evening meal with all the family normally takes about four hours, this evening it was twice that length.

Eventually, tiredness took over and I went to bed. The tropical sounds of the hillside and the soporific effect of the tequila soon put me to sleep and for eight hours I slept like a baby. The next day I spend the morning looking around the hacienda and the area I had known so well for so long. Eugene now had a much safer car with new shock absorbers and breaks, the hacienda had a refrigerator, and Marcia had sufficient dressmaking material to keep her occupied making dresses for the next few months.

Three weeks in the hills went all too quickly and I had to consider returning – but to where? I had no real base in Panama. Since leaving the villa five months ago, I had hardly obtained work. Mr. Salcedo gave me some translating work, just sufficient to stop me using my capital. A more secure income was seemingly very elusive.

It was only three days before I was about to leave for Panama City when, by chance, Eugene mentioned that the visiting foreign tourists liked Colombian jewelry, especially emeralds; it was just the information I wanted to hear. If only

I could get to the Mexican Riviera, to Zihuatanejo, Puerto Vallarta, or Playa Mismaloya, and open a stall selling Colombian jewelry – emerald jewelry – I might have just the possibilities of a new career. That was the start of my Mexican adventure.

The next three days were hectic. Telephone calls to Mr. Salcedo were successful and he arranged Mexican work permits for Marcia, Eugene, and myself, and with the help of my family, we arranged a supply of emerald jewelry. This would form the basis of our new endeavor.

Thinking about it, I would expect that wealthy Americans would be very interested in buying this beautiful stone. After all, emeralds are perhaps the most beautiful of all precious stones and command prices much higher than equivalent diamonds. The Colombian mountains are rich in emeralds. Regrettably, their exploitation has not been undertaken in a truly commercial way.

The next thing was to make sure that jewelry pieces were available; quite a task in itself, requiring considerable effort. Of course, the very beautiful large stones would fetch the most money and would sell well, especially at our competitive prices. With them, it is quite likely that a very profitable trade could be developed. During the cutting of the stones, a large number of smaller pieces are produced and these can also be skillfully designed and fabricated into jewelry that would be considerably cheaper, and perhaps an even bigger market might be possible. The whole of my family was now becoming involved, making sure that a good supply of jewelry would be available.

At 5 a.m., I alighted from a Panamanian tanker at Puerto

Vallarta. The quay was quiet, as I walked along in the direction of the town. My first task was to find a reasonable base from which I could work; then I would send for Marcia and Eugene. Playa Mismaloya was just the place to set up my first stall. Although not easily accessible from the land, Playa Mismaloya is frequently visited by all types of sea travelers. The jewelry soon arrived, and with the permission of the Puerto Vallarta authorities, I started my business. Eugene was correct, the tourists, especially the Americans, loved them. My stall was always surrounded, and within three days I had to cable for more supplies. If this was to continue, Marcia, Eugene, and I would soon be very rich.

If tourists were a good source of income on Playa Mismaloya, what would it be like in Acapulco? Soon I would know. Two months later, I found a site at the corner of the old market in Acapulco and there I set up a stall.

Looking at Bunny, I said, 'You are now up-to-date with my life story, for it was here in Acapulco that I first met you.'

Sitting on an original Mexican veranda, Bunny and Big Daddy Golding were fascinated by my story. It was now dusk and the blood-red sun was setting over the ocean. Its powerful light was forming golden halos around the strands of purple-blue clouds. By the minute, the colors were developing; initially, they were cool tinted colors against the blue sky, and then the warm oranges and reds entered the picture, changing to reds and purples before the crimson sun was finally extinguished as it sank into the almost jet-black sea. I had talked for nearly two hours, stopping only from time to time to enjoy the food and drink. Philippe and his wife produced some of the finest barbecued fish I've ever tasted. I dare not say how Big Daddy described it.

Bunny was impressed with the adventure of my short life. So was Big Daddy. Now, he was becoming more interested in its financial potential. 'Feliciano, the one thing you have done wrong,' he said, 'was to sell your stall in Playa Mismaloya when you moved to Acapulco. Each time you move on, you should leave a manager behind to keep the stall going. Then you have the profit from an increasing number of stalls.'

Baja California, Mexico

For three days, I was chauffeur and guide to Bunny and Big Daddy; each morning I would collect them from their hotel at about 10.30 and usually stayed with them until the small hours. They did not seem to want to sleep. To keep the market stall open, I asked an acquaintance, actually, the daughter of my landlord, if she would look after it for me. Maria Guadalupe[2] – she always used her full name – was just over seventeen years old and very capable of accepting my confidence in her, and she was ready to earn some money. She was of typical dark Spanish appearance and would have graced any New York fashion store; the smile on her face and the glint in eyes would surely attract more to the stall than ever I could. Once the men were there, the women would certainly do the rest and buy.

---

[2] Maria Guadalupe was named after Our Lady of Guadalupe, the patron Saint of Mexico and All The Americas. Our Lady of Guadalupe is the only authentic picture we have of the Virgin Mary. When asked by Saint Juan Diego, an Aztec Indian, in December 1532, at the request of the archbishop, the Virgin Mary said that she would imprint an image of herself on his tilmátli, a kind of cactus-fiber cloak. The image shows her with a brown face. The tunic still exists and is venerated in the Basilica of Our Lady Guadalupe in Mexico City, and it is claimed it shows no deterioration of its colours over 400 years.

Throughout the following days, I realized Big Daddy was right. I was being paid twice; once as a guide and once as stall-holder. If Maria Guadalupe would continue to look after the Acapulco stall, I could return to Playa Mismaloya and restart my stall there and then move it on with a manager to look after it.

It took only two months to establish stalls in ten different resorts. In each, I made a young lady its manager and put Maria Guadalupe in overall charge. She visited them once each week, checking on the stock and audited their accounts. Back in Cartagena, Marcia and Eugene were pushed to the limit to cope with supplies for all of the stalls. Another of my sisters, Maria, and her husband, Petro, were now helping. Also, Eugene was following Big Daddy's advice and had bought a new taxi and now had an assistant to drive the old one.

Maria Guadalupe was marvelous. She took to organizing the market stalls as if she had been a trained businesswoman. She organized all the staff and ensured the stalls were all well stocked. Again, on Big Daddy's advice and with the help of Mr. Salcedo, we made it a legal company, with Maria Guadalupe owning one-tenth of the company.

In two years, we owned all the market stalls in Acapulco, Zihuatanejo, Puerto Vallarta, and Playa Mismaloya, and many more. All the stallholders worked for Inca Inc. (Acapulco) as we then became known, and Maria Guadalupe set up our headquarters in a new office block in Acapulco – next to the Las Brisas Hotel where Bunny and Big Daddy usually stayed.

All my family in Cartagena were involved. Marcia was in charge of Inca Inc. (Cartagena), the jewelry supply company. It was only five years since returning from England and now all my family was involved – all enjoying our newfound wealth. Everybody worked on a wage plus commission basis. The harder they worked the more they earned. Central Americans are naturally hard workers.

I have now seen *The Night of the Iguana* many times, and I still find it just as interesting as I did two years ago when I first watched it with Bunny and Big Daddy. If it had not been for that film and the way it attracted so many Americans to the Pacific coast of Mexico, all wanting to catch a glimpse of the stars involved, I don't think my commercial ventures in Mexico would have started, let alone progressed in the way that they had. My priestly vacation never really left me and I was still in contact with Fr. John in England; whilst I suppose I could now re-enter the seminary, my life had become completely re-orientated into the business world and I wondered if I should. It is only occasionally that I think about it. Watching *The Night of the Iguana* usually brings it back to me.

Bunny and Big Daddy are still in contact with me and I still act as their guide when they return to Mexico. Mr. Salcedo ensured that my Mexican citizenship was in-order and his law company handles all of my legal work. With Maria Guadalupe now firmly in charge, I began to leave all the day-to-day running to her and to travel more and more in Central America, becoming very fond of Costa Rica. Why Costa Rica, I am not at all certain, I suppose it is because when I am in Colombia I am reminded of that very troubled part of my life when I was involved in the drug trade. In many ways, I feel ashamed of myself for being involved, but at that time it was the only way my family could be financially supported. If I had not been involved in the drug trade, I would not have met Mrs. Lopez nor would I have met Bunny and Big Daddy. In all probability, my family would have been very much poorer and I am not at all certain that with my background I would have been accepted back into the seminary. I think my views about the drug trade remain the same, although I have to admit they do provide considerable work for some local people; who without it would be penniless. They may be infamous, but they always look after their people. I still feel strongly that they would not exist if it was not for the people who use drugs. Mostly the users are in wealthy countries and many of the users are themselves prosperous, but sadly many poor people are caught up in their use and this disturbs me. It was perhaps to get that out of my system that my interest in Costa Rica began; I just wanted to get away from Colombia.

On the few occasions, I visited Costa Rica in the past, I was particularly attracted to the people and the beauty of its coastline and its countryside. Of course, I frequently returned to see my family in Cartagena and I often met Maria Guadalupe, although I do not need to supervise her work for she is more talented than I am in the business world. We were not just making money – we were actually circulating money, into Colombia and particularly to some of the poor people there. The money was going to Colombia benefiting many people. My family certainly benefited. My participation in the drug trade, and I am not proud of that, made my family secure and all our money has stayed in Colombia. Our stalls, selling jewelry made from emeralds mined in Colombia, have generated a very large amount of work and the money has contributed to the Colombian economy. Without my first involvement in the drug trade, that part of their economy would been impossible. The big demand for drugs provides an enormous amount of work in Colombia, not only in the growing of cannabis but also in the industrial-scale processing of coca leaves into cocaine. Many people are involved in the industry and it would be economically quite disastrous for them if it was to stop. At least, with my ill-gotten gains, I was able to finance selling emerald jewelry which was beneficial to a very large number of people and it is not drug-based. I genuinely feel that there has been some good in what has happened.

Costa Rica and Coffee

I was now looking for somewhere to invest the profits of Inca Inc. (Acapulco) and Inca Inc. (Cartagena); diversification is what is needed was Big Daddy's advice.

It was whilst I was in Costa Rica that I decided to move into the coffee business. Coffee is a commodity that will always be needed. I knew very little about coffee; all I knew was that it is a very pleasant drink and something that I enjoy. I thought it would be straightforward; I would simply buy a plantation and let it go from there. That certainly was very naive and it came as a considerable surprise to me to find that I was not welcomed as a newcomer and even more of a surprise to me to find that, like the drug industry, coffee was governed by a cartel of existing plantation owners. The fact that there was a cartel involved made me very suspicious. It usually means that the natural commercial rules are not followed and that there could be considerable problems to surmount.

Maria Guadalupe was eager to diversify her efforts; she was interested in all forms of Central America trade, and joined me in Costa Rica. As always, Maria Guadalupe's advice was good and straight to the point. She quickly realized that with all-natural growing products there were good years, not so good years, and bad years Separating the production of coffee from its demand, she thought, was the key to commercial success – keeping the price constant was the route forward. We bought two more small plantations on the coast, not far from San José, and Maria Guadalupe sought technical advice on a new approach not yet followed by the other coffee plantations. It was to store the beans before final dispatch, blending and roasting. The University of Costa Rica in San José had been trying for some time to get the plantation owners interested in this approach, to no avail. They were simply happy to accept the rising price of coffee when the crop was poor offsetting the lower prices when the crop was good. Maria Guadalupe had other ideas. Costa Rica coffee was very popular and could always demand high prices. She and the University of Costa Rica were convinced that the more coffee the market produced the lower would be the price and the higher would then be its demand, all would then benefit. High demand would need a continuous supply, hence the need for storage of the beans.

Inca Inc. (Coffee) started to build large silos with carefully controlled atmospheres; this allowed the beans to be stored for over twelve months, long before the first signs of deterioration occurred. They were then be able to allow a good year to subsidize a poor one. With further research work at San José University, storage for longer periods would soon be possible. Inca Inc. (Coffee) was quick to sponsor these studies.

As each small plantation came on the market, Inca Inc. (Coffee) bought it. Soon they were one of the top ten plantation owners – only the larger ones were left. It was then that we first came across the coffee cartel owners. Our small acquisitions constantly outbid theirs – something that had never happened before. Not surprisingly, the cartel members were none too pleased and reacted against us.

One day, Maria Guadalupe was alone in our Costa Rican office. She had just arrived from Acapulco when six men entered. At first, she was not concerned; she had handled so-called tough men before.

Looking sternly at Maria Guadalupe. The leader said. 'Your storage system is interfering with the coffee prices and the cartel is not pleased. Recently, you held down the price of coffee during a poor yield year and that is not allowed. All coffee beans sold must be from that year's harvest – no other.' With that, one of the men took the ruler from her desk and used it to lift the hem of her skirt. For a moment, she froze. Then, just as he was proceeding to lift the hem further, she snatched the ruler from him, striking him a severe blow to the eye causing blood to flow profusely. The man's anger could hardly be contained. Fortunately for Maria Guadalupe, the other men intervened.

'Do as we say,' snarled the man with blood streaming down his face. 'We will be back.'

They did come back four months later – when they did, Maria Guadalupe was ready. Since the previous incident, she always came to the plantations accompanied by her brothers and cousins. On the afternoon the cartel thugs arrived, her brothers were in the office, as usual, looking more like clerks than bodyguards. Once inside the office, the cartel thugs moved immediately towards Maria Guadalupe, especially the one with the new scar above his left eye. He wasn't there to negotiate; he was out for revenge. Scarface attempted to grab Maria Guadalupe. Before he had made two steps forward, he was overpowered by her brothers as also were his associates. Maria Guadalupe, without saying a word, took a pair of scissors from her drawer and immediately cut off Scarface's tie. He was now not at all certain what was going to happen next. She then, in seconds, she rendered his shirt and trousers into ribbons. 'Don't come here again until I invite you; next time it will not only be your clothes I will attack.'

White-faced and shaking, he was ready to leave, and his minders certainly did not want to hang around. Intimidation had not worked. Marie Guadalupe was now always ready with more of her Mexican family. It was not uncommon to see the cartel thugs leaving the plantations naked as they ran to their vehicles, often immobilized with sandy carburetors.

***

It was late in the afternoon, as the light was fading, when Feliciano and Maria Guadalupe entered the office of the coffee cartel in San José. They had been invited for lunch, but Maria Guadalupe had other plans. She wanted to make sure that we were in no way indebted to them; rather it should be the other way. We had simply ignored their lunch invitation, giving the impression we would arrive when we wanted to. It was now 4:35 p.m. and twenty sullen-faced men were still in the boardroom of the cartel, of the Costa Rica Coffee Corporation.

Señor Costello spoke first. 'Welcome, Feliciano, and Maria Guadalupe. May I call you by your first names? After all, I hope that very soon we will be partners.

'Please do.'

Señor Costello continued, 'we all know that Costa Rican coffee is the best in the world and our production is very good;

furthermore, there is enough profit for all our plantation owners, who also are all very close friends.'

Maria Guadalupe replied, 'we are more than happy to be friends, although some of your men have tried to be a little too friendly.' Her dark eyes shone as she stood up to the whole of the cartel. All eyes were on her, partly because of her beauty and partly because of her imposing appearance and her strong words.

'Well, I'm sorry about that and I can guarantee it will not happen again.' That was probably the first time Señor Costello had apologized in front of the cartel and certainly never before to a lady. Maria Guadalupe had played a trump card in the negotiations, making sure that the cartel started by first apologizing to her.

'I'll get straight to the point,' said Señor Costello. 'We have resisted developments to even out the cost of coffee; we make more money in the relatively poor harvests than the good ones and we wanted it to stay that way.'

Maria Guadalupe spoke. 'I can understand that, but we must always remember that coffee drinkers provide our profits and with Africa providing very good coffee, soon we will not be able to sell our coffee at prices dictated only by our market. World prices will be the deciding factor. We are preparing for that day.'

'There are other methods,' said Señor Costello. 'We could buy some of the African plantations or even buy their beans.'

'If we don't remember those who drink coffee, we will lose our income,' insisted Maria Guadalupe.

Looking around the table, I could see the faces of the cartel members and particularly their eyes; they were very intent on what Maria Guadalupe was saying. Relatively few members were looking glum and only one looked annoyed – Scarface.

Señor Costello was trying to be reasonable; he pointed out that the cartel was long-standing and its members owned ninety percent of the plantations. 'We may be somewhat old-fashioned; nevertheless, we have prospered and our members want it to stay that way.'

'I understand that; we are not dictating your prices, as you say, we own only one-tenth of the total plantation area. What we have done is to ensure a constant price for our coffee when production is both good and when it falls. We are very happy to live with you; we are not asking you to change. We will see in time who is correct.

Finally,' said Maria Guadalupe, 'we are willing to buy more plantations and we are prepared to pay the market price.'

With that, we left after shaking hands with each member of the board. I watched them all acknowledging Maria Guadalupe who was all smiles, and I believed she had won their approval; only one kept his face stern. However, he did not look down at her skirt; what was he thinking!

'What did you think of the meeting?' I asked Maria Guadalupe as we drove back to the plantation.

'I don't trust them. They were far too friendly and they were almost accommodating. They were just testing us.'

'I think so too. We must be very careful and especially you, you must watch out for Scarface.'

'Don't worry, my brothers will protect me.'

Our plan was not to change. We continued to build up our storage system, buying up all the surplus beans we could.

Whilst I looked after the coffee plantations, Maria Guadalupe was spending most of her time in Mexico. We were successful in purchasing three more estates, in each case from cartel members. Now we were the largest single coffee company in Costa Rica with about twenty percent of the country's plantations.

Scarface never forgave Maria Guadalupe. Twice he attempted to attack her and each time he was repelled by her brothers. On the third occasion, he attacked her whilst she was in Acapulco; thinking she would not be protected there. Late one night, he followed her home and, with three of his buddies, he grabbed her. As they wrestled together, she snatched his knife and thrust it deep into his groin. At the sight of blood, his friends fled, leaving him to the mercy of Maria Guadalupe. For a moment, she was about to stab him again. She held back, taking care not to send for help too quickly. When she thought he had suffered enough she left the scene and only then made an anonymous call for an ambulance. No charges were preferred against Maria Guadalupe. Scarface should not have been in Mexico and his final indignity was being deported to Costa Rica and then having to face his colleagues, a physically broken man. Scarface did not walk properly again. Life for Maria Guadalupe was now quieter and much safer.

Next year, an unheard-of thing happened; almost all the country's flowering coffee bushes suffered frost damage and a year of beans were lost. If that was not all, a coffee beetle attacked the bushes and many had to be cut down and burned. The smell of burning wood imbued the whole of the countryside. It was a disaster so bad that many of the cartels wanted to sell up and leave. The value of the Inca Inc. (Coffee) stored beans rocketed, and with the profit they were able to buy eight of the remaining sixteen plantations. Inca Inc. (Coffee) now owned three-quarters of the plantations in Costa

Rica. The final irony was that many of the stored beans had been purchased from the cartel members at very low prices during the previous year's plentiful harvest.

Maria Guadalupe and I met monthly. She was now the chief executive of Inca Inc. (Coffee) and made most of the day-to-day decisions, yet she remained only a minority shareholder in the company not wishing to increase her holding. She was simply satisfied with the bonuses she received. Together we owned all of the Inca Inc. Empire; we had no other shareholders nor did we want any. Our cash flow was very secure and we had no debts.

Maria Guadalupe and I showed no signs of romance between us, our friendship was firm and strong and completely platonic.

Back Home in Colombia

I was now visiting Colombia more and more. We planned to augment Inca Inc. (Coffee) with our Colombian coffee plantations and develop a bean storage system in Colombia. This might not be so easy with the drug cartels still dominating almost every aspect of life, including coffee.

I had no allegiances to the drug cartels. I had not disclosed any information to the British authorities whilst I was in prison and now, seven years later, their trade was continuing to increase. I was not interested in invading their privacy. I did not agree with the drug industry, but users were just as guilty as the pushers, in my mind. I was, however, very interested in the Colombia economy, and its agricultural and mineral development, especially coffee and emeralds. The careful development of the coffee, emeralds and the gold industry would be bound to increase the prosperity of the nation and this would be to the benefit all.

Unfortunately, the drug trade was causing many peripheral and adverse problems to Colombia, particularly concerning its ability to trade with other countries. The US was trying very hard to stop the importation of these harmful drugs, and was considering banning all trade with drug-producing countries. If the Colombian coffee, emerald and gold industries were not allowed to export to the US, the country's prosperity would fall sharply. So far, Marcia had managed all our Colombian emerald businesses without any problems. The cartels had not caused her any difficulties and the government was happy with the jewelry exports she had arranged. Would it be the same for coffee?

All in all, Inca Inc. had over five thousand people working for them. Most would have been out of work if it had not been for them. A survey by an independent company, commissioned by the government, concluded that they were paid nearly thirty times the average Colombian workers wage. This did not tell the whole story since it must be remembered that half of the available workforce in Colombia had no work at all.

***

I had just arrived in Cartagena on one of my visits and was staying at the Imperial Hotel in the old part of the city. Usually, I would stay at our family hacienda; today it was convenient to stay at the Imperial Hotel.

I had just dined in the restaurant and was now taking coffee and brandy on the veranda, whilst at the same time watching the late nightlife of the city. It was a little cooler now that darkness had descended. The streets were dimly lit, relying mainly on the flickering lights in the shop windows for illumination. Although I felt tired, I was in no hurry to retire. The friendly murmurs of the young couples, and the not so young, as they strolled through the square, gave the city an almost eternal feeling. In the past, I have always thought that the best time of the day was in the morning; this evening, out on the veranda with the sweet floral perfume still lingering, I was beginning to wonder if I might well change my mind.

I had just ordered more coffee when two men accompanied by a very attractive young lady approached me. They were all strangers to me, and they addressed me as Señor Solaccio. 'May I introduce myself,' said the young lady. 'My name is Jacinta[3] and I am the general secretary of the Christian Liberal Democrats and an assistant to El Presidente. May I introduce my colleagues José and Isi.'

We shook hands. 'Please sit down and join me for coffee – I've just ordered a fresh supply. Señorita, can I have three more cups, please.' For a few minutes, we exchanged pleasantries whilst I poured out four cups of steaming coffee. After asking permission, the two men lit up small cigars. Who they were, and what they wanted, I had no idea, and they did not appear to be in a hurry tell me. They were very smartly dressed and spoke to me in a somewhat measured manner.

Jacinta was a very attractive young lady and I was somewhat surprised to see that she held such a senior political position. José and Isi were quite content to let her lead the conversation. She paused for a little while as she inhaled the intoxicating mixture of coffee and 'evening' fragrances. I could see the electric lights reflecting in her dark eyes, enhancing her beauty even more. I'm sure her looks had not done her one scrap of harm as she must have grappled against male domination to achieve the post she now held.

---

[3] Jacinta was named after St Jacinta de Jesus Marto the youngest of the three children the Virgin Mary appeared to at Fatima in 1917. She died at the very young age of ten from the Spanish flu epidemic that struck Europe.

She then spoke. 'I rarely travel outside Central America, but the traveling I have done has always made me think what a great country Colombia is and how we must look after it.'

As Jacinta paused, Isi took up the conversation. 'I believe you have spent much of your life in the hills and the mountains of Colombia as indeed have I, and it is there where both of us have seen nature and wildlife, the detail of which many scientists would love to see. It was only when I was a student at the University in Barcelona that I started to realize the good fortune of a Colombian inheritance. My mother, many years ago, met a visiting explorer and fell in love with him. She was then a very young girl only fifteen years old. Well, I was the fruit of their short passionate love affair. I never saw my father; he left very soon after I was conceived. My very young mother with the help of her parents and her wider family brought me up and gave me the best education they could manage. Her wish was that I should have an education similar to that of my biological father and she set about achieving this. Later, she married and her new husband helped her in that task. I still remember very clearly the happiness in her eyes as she kissed me after the degree congregation at Barcelona University; it was from this university that my father had graduated.

'I must stop; I'm sure I am boring you, but your remarks and those of Jacinta about the beauty of Colombia always make me think of my mother.'

José remained quite silent; he was content to just puff on his cigar whilst sipping coffee. We were now on yet another pot.

They certainly wanted to talk about something; what it was I was not sure. I don't think it simply was the pleasures and beauty of Cartagena or Colombia or was it? The way the evening had gone so far gave me the feeling it was one of those occasions when they were preparing to ask a question and were concerned that the answer might not be what they wanted to hear.

I said very little, and they were content to talk. The evening was peaceful and with the gentle airflow through the square and the delicate perfume of the flowers together with the soporific effect of the coffee and cognac, all in all, it was very pleasant. There were strangers to me, but somehow that did not seem to matter.

Jacinta stood up and walked to the end of the veranda; for a while, she looked across the square. The lights opposite cast a gentle illumination in her direction and I could see her outline – she looked very attractive. After a few minutes, she returned and sat on the cane settee just opposite me causing her overlapping skirt to part; slowly she re-arranged it. As she made herself comfortable it was as if she was more interested in what she was about to say rather than her appearance. She seemed quite oblivious of her skirt parting again. Was she about to tell me the reason for their visit?

I remarked. 'As pleasant as the evening has been, I'm sure you did not come here just to take coffee with me.' The waiter had now removed the coffee cups and placed a tray of home-made chocolates before us. I passed them around, waiting for their reply.

José and Isi looked in the direction of Jacinta.

'When I visit a restaurant in the old city on an evening like this, I think I am lucky to live and work in Cartagena, at least for part of my time.' She paused and readjusted her skirt making sure this time that the side of the wrap overran centrally down her left leg. 'We have summertime all year round and peace and prosperity to match it. The problem is that this is only true for some of the people of Colombia and it should be true for all.'

I could see she was speaking from her heart.

'We have a large fertile country, a mineral-rich country, a historical country and a country with people who are longing to be freed from some of the worst poverty in Central America. It is time we changed and made better use of all our resources for the benefit of everybody.'

'I can only agree with that,' I replied, 'Is not that the aim of all politicians; a rhetorical question, but it is one that required immediately answering.'

'If they say that, do they mean it?' Now it was Jacinta who was asking a rhetorical question. 'Our climate and our land should grow harvests wholly acceptable to the world.' There was silence; we all knew exactly what she was referring to. She went on. 'At first, the growing of cannabis was for medicinal purposes; now it is more than a simple natural herb. Initially, it helped a poor nation live within itself, now it is a very different story – its uses have become much more widespread and its addictive properties have increased its value, which has quickly been exploited. Cocaine and heroin are in a similar position; world trade and wider individual traveling have quickly spread the use of these drugs and, in so doing, rapidly increased the profits that can be made from them. Our country has two economies – only one we admit to. The other, although very much in the official shadow, has far-reaching effects on all our lives, yet it is directed by mercenary leaders with no representation from its people.

'If that is not bad enough,' said Jacinta, 'now we have the

President of the United States saying that the whole world should boycott all Colombian produce, coffee, emeralds and gold until the export of drugs to the US are halted.'

'I understand your concern. How can I help? I only know about trading in coffee and emeralds and, what is more, I would certainly gain if the US were to stop buying Colombian coffee – already the price of Costa Rican coffee has risen on the rumor.'

It was now quite late; the cathedral clock had struck one o'clock. However, life on the streets had not changed. The cool of the evening had brought out more and more people and the lateness was adding romance and not urgency to the small hours. Calling the waitress over I ordered more coffee and the men had another glass of cognac.

'Here in Colombia, we have been watching how successful you have been with the Costa Rica coffee cartel and we have noted how all your coffee plantation workers are now much happier with their working conditions. Likewise, we know how your Mexican enterprise has benefited the Colombian emerald industry, and this has been enjoyed by all of your workers. I know your sister Marcia very well, and I can vouch from first hand that these benefits are real.'

The fresh coffee had now arrived and I poured Jacinta a cup. She inhaled the aromatic fragrance for a while, and I wasn't certain if she was going to speak or whether I should reply. Neither happened for what seemed an eternity – we just sat thinking. Then she spoke. 'We have also noticed that your workers have benefited equally from your success; it has not been at their expense.'

'Thank you, that pleases me greatly. I agree with your view; after all, our people are our greatest resource, and I always try to remember that.'

We had now been talking for nearly three hours, and I was still no wiser as to why Jacinta and her colleagues had called on me. Certainly, it was not just to talk, no matter how pleasant that had been.

Looking directly at me Jacinta suddenly said, 'It is time we changed our approach to the way our country is being run – we need a new direction.'

Politics were not my forte and it was with some considerable surprise and incredulity that I listened to Jacinta as she asked me to consider leading the Christian Liberal Democrats. For a while I was speechless. It was the last thing on my mind. Quite frankly, my only interest was to ensure that my businesses did well, not because I wanted the profit; no, it was because I knew that many people depended on me, and I did not want to let them down.

Eventually, when I felt I could speak, I said quite simply, 'No, quite frankly, I am surprised that you should ask me and, of course, I am honored to have your confidence, but I have no experience in politics and my experience of life generally is hardly appropriate.'

'Please don't say no – please think again. We not only want a new leader. We need a new government and a new prime minister.'

'But I have no experience. In any event, I have been part of the drug trade – in fact, quite a big part. I was responsible for much of its expansion into Europe and of developing its money laundering system. I am just as guilty as any of the members of the cartel.'

'Yes, I understand, but it was purely because of the circumstances you found yourself in; immediately you could, you broke away from it. That has happened with many of our politicians. They too have taken a practical approach to their existing situation. I think all of us will continue to be involved in the drug trade for a long time – it is all a matter of keeping it under control. Many of the poor people of South America gain some rewards for working for the cartels and also from producing small quantities of cocaine on their farms. But the present situation is something we cannot accept; the profits from the drug barons are being laundered overseas with no benefit to our country. Our economy will probably get worse. Defiantly it will if we cannot make sure that our legal products enter the world markets – coffee especially. It is here that we think you are probably the only person in South America who can help our countries develop an acceptable economy from which the poor of all our countries will benefit. You have the greatest of all political experience and ability, you can motivate people to work, and you know how to make them prosperous. That is exactly what a prime minister does. I know you cannot decide right now after only just one late-night meeting, but please do not dismiss it out of hand. Please, can we meet again, perhaps tomorrow?

Jacinta went on, 'the political picture in Colombia is slowly changing and its economy is starting to expand. A poor country cannot readily turn its back on any part of its development whether it is good or bad. The drug cartels have been very successful and at least some of our people have benefited. However, things are now a little different – no, more than that – they are fundamentally different. The cartels' success has been so great and the profits so large that they have started to invest their money in many other countries of the world. The diversification of their wealth is now to the detriment of our nation; no longer is the Colombian economy the sole beneficiary. Drugs are leaving the country, but the money is not returning. It is going to Switzerland, Bermuda, the Bahamas, and many other banking nations. Without this money appearing in the Colombian banks, our national deficit is increasing and the value of the peso is falling. Today, the future looks far from good.

'The Bogotá government had less than one year to run before the next elections so now is the time for action. The cartels are pragmatic – if the drug trade is allowed, they will continue to give the government support – a feature that applies to almost all of the 'drug governments' of the Americas. The US Government is not happy with this. Law and order in the United States is deteriorating and drugs are judged to be one of the principal reasons for this. World opinion is changing against the drug economy and it is now time that the shadowy *entente cordiale* between the Colombian Government and the drug cartels was severed. The cartels are not likely to allow that, they will fight it.'

Back in South America

El Presidente was more than familiar with the problems of Colombia. For a decade, he had strived to look after all the people of his country – the obvious task of a president and something that was more easily said than done. Colombia's rich natural resources played little part in the development of its economy. A much more sinister and dark economy constantly plagued him. Putting aside the evils of drugs, for it is an economy of sorts, it's production was still not a good reason for taking over all the potentially profitable agricultural land; land that could have been used for growing bananas, cocoa, coffee and corn – produce that would benefit all its people, not just a few. If only the overall agricultural industry was allowed to fully develop, a large workforce would be involved, contributing considerably to the general welfare of all.

The drug cartels cause many other problems, but until an adequate alternative system of utilizing the vast natural resources in Colombia is developed, they will dominate. Alternatives put forward by the government that do not help the cartels are often vetoed or prevented, in some way. With the election coming, there was once more an opportunity for the president to try and persuade the people to help him bring about changes.

El Presidente and his staff were working very hard on the party's election manifesto. As usual, Jacinta was a leading light in many of the discussions. Not only was it necessary to put forward a realistic and practical manifesto, but it was necessary to think very carefully about how it could be implemented, and who should lead the new government as prime minister. Jacinta had spent a lot of her time looking around for a suitable person and kept coming back to the same man – the brother of her school friend, Marcia Solaccio. He and his staff had been particularly successful in coping with the coffee cartels in Costa Rica and also in parts of Colombia. She had convinced El Presidente that Señor Feliciano Solaccio was just the man to lead a new government as prime minister, possibly with some help from Maria Guadalupe.

The cartels' power was something El Presidente was more than aware of, and most certainly, he was not part of it. However, he suspected that many of his officials probably were. Unbeknown to him, his own son-in-law, Alfredo, the minister of finance, was an active leading member. He also had suspicions about his own two sons; both were leaders of their respective councils in Bogotá and Cartagena and both had very expensive wives. He also knew that, secretly, the CIA had very close contacts with the Bogotá government. They had agents in the department of the interior and the treasury department and they probably knew more than El Presidente about the cartel members in his government. Needless to say, the cartels countered with snoopers in the US Embassy.

Cartel-manipulated countries have unusual economies – often rich in underutilized natural resources. They are frequently just ripe for the production of drugs – drugs that generate immense wealth for some. In America, countries like Colombia and Mexico, the term *poor* has to be very carefully defined and certainly very cautiously used. As far as natural wealth is concerned, South America, as a whole, is extremely fortunate; it is blessed with ample natural resources, making them far from being poor. Its people are hard-working and its climate is just right for tropical growth; in the mountains, tropical rainforests are extraordinarily lush, making all the ground around equally fertile. In addition to all this, there is an enviable array of wildlife of all kinds There are parts of South America where only plant and animal life live. The countries are so vast the rainforests have not yet been fully explored, and this is at a time when man has already stood on the moon. In the cultivated areas, coffee beans, the nectar of the rich, grow extremely well – both the delicate Arabica beans and their more plentiful Robusta beans; they all enjoy the climate, as do corn, cocoa and bananas. Additionally, there is one of the greatest treasures of all – spectacular emeralds. They are mined from its earth, and with the plentiful deposits of gold, they adorn the rich and famous on all five continents of the world. Not to be forgotten, the land yields other valuable primeval products, such as oil and coal; formed many millions of years ago from the pre-historic prolific foliage of forests and vegetation.

Then why are they so poor? Sadly, this is the question often asked of many so-called third world countries. Quite simply, its leaders have not correctly carried out the duties entrusted to them. It has not always been their fault. Often it was the colonizing countries that have taken all and given very little in return. For the privileged few, the standard of living in

Colombia, as in most of South America, is very high. Careful examination shows government officials are usually the main members of this privileged few – something that is true throughout the entire world, particularly in third world nations. Corruption is often rife and often increases when there is a threat of political or social change of any kind.

Visiting South America today confirms to the traveler that times are changing and Colombia is no exception. The cities of Bogotá and Medellin are now entering fully into the twentieth century. But travel only a few kilometers out of the center of the city and the picture changes. Picture – is the appropriate word to use, for although the landscape, with all its mountainous regions, is breathtakingly and dramatically beautiful, close examination reveals a less attractive image. It shows the mountain people have only modest living standards. They are truly poor, not only in the trappings that modern-day life often calls affluence, but also in the basic necessities of life including shelter, food, health care and education. The situation will worsen if export trade is prevented.

For months, the Bogotá government has been watching as the world price of coffee rises. Normally this would have been something to rejoice about, but not now. The government is fully aware that the real reason for this is that pretty soon there will be a complete world boycott of all Colombian coffee.

United States Embargo

on Colombian Coffee

The price of Colombian coffee had fallen to its lowest level ever on the futures exchange market. The President of the United States has just signed a bill to ban the importation of Colombian coffee to the US. This immediately made coffee exports from countries such as Jamaica and Kenya move to all-time highs, in Costa Rica they were soaring. The US government, knowing that the bulk of drugs, in particular cannabis, cocaine and heroin, originate in Colombia and Mexico, was now going to use a trade embargo as one way of stopping this undesirable inflow of drugs into their country. Boycotting trade was bound to have a severe effect on the economy of any coffee-exporting country, and more than anything would show them that they should act against their drug cartels. Attacking the economies of these two countries, particularly their coffee exports, was a powerful tool. The US itself would not suffer from shortage – their needs could be satisfied with imports from other more reliable countries of the world.

The Colombian government feared that this embargo

would inevitably influence the result of their upcoming election, now only a few months away. A complete boycott of Colombian coffee would devastate further their already poor living standards. It was not surprising, therefore, that there was real concern in El Presidente's residence. The problem with elections in Central and South America is that they are very unpredictable and are often both internally and externally manipulated. Often this means that for a serving government to continue in power it is likely to be controlled by its shadowy masters. El Presidente was trying hard to have a government based on a real and acceptable economy consisting of a mixture of agriculture and the controlled utilization of all its natural resources. They should not be artificially influenced by a criminal-based power, particularly one manipulated by the cartels. He believed it was possible, in his country, to have a good economy – one which would increase the standard of living of all its citizens, an economy they could all be proud of and one that would find a very respectable place in the Americas, and in the whole world.

The office of the president was never quiet and even today, although it was a national holiday, there was plenty of activity preparing for the election. El Presidente's aides had been trying to get hold of some key members of the government – all were out of the city with their families. Although they were all probably within a few minutes away from El Presidente's office, they just were not inclined to answer their telephones or respond to their bleepers. Each minister had the attitude that El Presidente would be able to contact sufficient of their colleagues to allow a reasonable consensus to be reached on any topic. For many of them, ministerial duties were judged to be a necessary evil; enjoying the good life was the main objective.

The US had now made it quite clear that countries producing drugs must not send them to the US. Not only must they cease, but they must also show that they have stopped by destroying their cannabis and coca plantations – a real tall order and quite a formidable task in itself, since most of these countries are vast and their governments are not fully aware of exactly what is happening in some of the remote parts of their lands. The Colombian air force was insufficient to carry out a comprehensive survey – the US was assisting with satellite reconnaissance. Even then, in some jungle regions, it was very difficult to identify some of the smaller drug-growing areas together with their hidden industrial processing plants and distribution centers.

With the might of the enormous US economy behind the trade boycott, its effects would inevitably be very damaging to all of the exports from Colombia and Mexico – not just coffee. The drug problem in the United States was extremely serious and was having a major effect on its people, on crime, and on the whole of its social society; the government was very concerned. The United States was not going to stand for that and would take appropriate action necessary against any country supplying drugs to them. They simply had to stop.

The governments of both Colombia and Mexico were forced to agree to the US demands and had instructed their armies to find these growing areas and destroy them. When the order was given in Colombia, El Presidente could see it made many of his cabinet members uneasy. All agreed to the order, although some argued strongly that they should not submit to the US government's demands. After all, Colombia was almost half the size of the United States and should be strong enough to repel their interference.

In response to the United States' demands, just before the feast of Our Lady of Guadalupe, on the 12th of December, the government ordered an attack on the main drug-producing areas. It had taken three months of discussion and careful planning to ensure it could and would happen. At the presidential cabinet meeting, Alfredo reported to El Presidente on the recent attempts of the government forces to reduce the production of drugs; he claimed it was likely to be successful.

***

Later that night at his home, Alfredo held another meeting significantly attended by more than half those present at the presidential cabinet meeting, plus many of the top echelons of the military and police, all now casually dressed. The cartel members were everywhere! The plan was, in some way, to neutralize the decisions of the morning's cabinet meeting. It was now 11 p.m. and the burning heat of the day had cooled to a pleasant 25°. For two hours, they dined by the floodlit swimming pool, eating scrumptious food and drinking fine wine. As they dined and chatted with each other, several bikini-clad young girls mingled with them. They were hardly noticed by the guests – mostly they were far more interested in their conversation, which would stop if they were approached.

At one o'clock, Alfredo's guests reconvened to further develop their pre-dinner discussions. Alfredo opened the discussion. 'We are all aware that today's decision to destroy the coca and cannabis plantations could affect all our lives. We all have an enjoyable life, experiencing standards of living much higher than that of our parents and standards that are not possible on our salaries alone.'

He looked around the table at the assenting fellow ministers and guests; all knew that this was something with which they could fully concur. Even those in the more rural parts of the country, where the standard of living might still be low, had benefited from both legitimate and illegitimate trade. 'Today, we must have a Colombia that decides its destiny, and this evening we must lead these decisions. Tomorrow we must make sure that this does not change.' Again, he paused, and again the gathering acceded to his words. 'El Presidente has his duties to perform and he must be seen to be fully acting in the way that people would like him to act. We must help him to carry out his duties and follow his instructions in the most appropriate manner.' All present were clear of the meaning of this coded message 'appropriate manner' and nobody had any illusions about the true situation. All were enjoying the life that politicians in the Central Americas were renowned for. It was well known that illicit payments for favors could enhance the wealth and power of the 'privileged' few. The government ministers were well rewarded for the help they gave the cartels. Tonight's party was arranged to demonstrate this and it certainly did that and did it very well. 'No minister could live this affluent life on ministerial pay alone. Give me your backing and I am sure it will last.' Alfredo hardly needed to have asked for it; for he knew it would be forthcoming. All knew that the cartels would supply the money to finance whatever action was necessary.

Despite his apparent confidence, deep-down, Alfredo was uncertain as to whether he should be pleased or not with what was happening, for he sensed there could be problems. US interference with the internal affairs of Colombia was now happening and this was likely to damage his credibility with the cartels.

***

Nassau was the venue for a routine meeting of the cartels. They recognized the popularity of El Presidente and were not putting forward their candidate at the oncoming election. However, the present prime minister was not well, and a new candidate was required for the post. The cartel had their ideas. Señor Marcio, who had played a big part in developing the spread of the drug industry in the USA, was just the man. It was time to release him from US work and move him into national politics. In any event, it was their policy not to leave anyone in an important position for too long. By that process, only a few people knew who was really in charge and who was directing policies – policies they could change frequently to avoid detection. The cartel members were beginning to think Señor Marcio was getting to be a little too powerful. Yes, Señor Marcio would be ideal as prime minister – that would be the right place for him.

They were not aware of El Presidente's plan and the agreement with the Liberal Christian Democrats, or the plan to ask Señor Feliciano Solaccio to be his running mate as prime minister.

Back in Bogotá.

El Presidente the US Ambassador.

For the next week, the smell of hillsides burning was everywhere. The difficult decision had been taken. With El Presidente receiving reports from the army that the cannabis, heroin and cocaine plantations were burning, he immediately summoned US embassy officials to the palace to be told officially that the US President's wishes had been followed. El Presidente was not happy that he had been forced to follow policies and directions of the US President, although he was happy to see the possible beginning of the end of the drug problem. Colombia could now look forward to a more peaceful economy, even though the complete end of the drug problem was not yet nigh. Problems would continue to remain within the government; however, the government's position was now clear and unambiguous.

The meeting was very cordial. All knew very well that El Presidente had been a fellow Harvard student of the US ambassador and they still enjoyed each other's company. Later, they met privately. 'El Presidente, I am not at all sure what you're saying is correct,' said the US ambassador.

'Recent satellite pictures indicate only limited destruction. US surveillance photographs show that only some areas are burning; most remain untouched.' There was silence. Both men looked at each other for a long time and both knew exactly the real situation. They had known each other for many years and neither would knowingly deceive the other; their friendship had been built upon mutual trust. The ambassador's expression showed concern – he knew his friend had real problems.

The ambassador had to help and respond or his friend would be severely at risk. 'I'm pleased to hear of the action you have taken, El Presidente. I will tell the White House immediately. The American people and the people of the world are looking forward to enjoying the fruits of our peaceful corporation, not least to your delicious coffee and your wonderful emeralds and diamonds.' Both men were thinking rapidly as to what to say next.

El Presidente stood up and walked slowly around his desk to the ambassador. Smiling and touching him on the shoulder, he then walked slowly to the table on the other side of the room. After filling two crystal glasses with ice, he poured from a decanter. Beckoning, he said, 'It's never too early to have a drink with a friend.' They walked through the slightly open glass doors and onto the patio. 'Look,' said El Presidente. 'There is no better view in the whole of the Americas. It is a view that all Colombians should be able to see and enjoy and I intend to see that it happens.'

The ambassador sipped at the iced bourbon – the cold strong liquid lingered in his throat. He felt he must make a response, but what? For a while, they stood and looked at the wonder's nature had made for them – wonders unprepared and untouched by man.

El Presidente looked carefully at the ambassador. 'William,' he said, 'it does not surprise me at all that I have been deceived by my ministers. It will be a long time before we have a government in South America that is not tainted by greed. Colombia is a country where illicit trade has dominated its economy for decades and it will not readily change; life in Latin America is just like that. My task is to please everybody, protect the country's economy and especially look after all of its people. The latter is the most difficult and the most important. William, you must tell the White House how difficult life is in the Colombian countryside. If we cannot sell our coffee then the people will starve – it's as simple as that. I do not control the drug industry, and what is more I probably never will. Whilst there are users, in capitalistic countries, it will continue to exist, there will always be a drug trade. The users are not in Colombia. I know this does not encapsulate your countries view, which simply is the opposite, it is untrue and it is unreasonable. We will have to wait and see how it all finally ends, as certainly it will one day; in the meanwhile, we will do our best to control it and I must look after my people.'

The ambassador was quiet as he looked at his friend and at the scene before him; politics and diplomatic service, especially in South America, were full of opposing factions and contradictions. Life is not straightforward and it has to be seen, and experienced to be fully believed. El Presidente was a good man who cared for his people, but he had to be practical. What else could he do? Politicians have only so much power and it can be taken away in a moment.

'You know, every day, in my attempts to make Colombia great and feed its subjects, I must push my ideologies to one side; I know that is necessary. It is a long time since I first realized how true is the Machiavellian and sometimes Jesuit quoted, saying, 'that the ends do justify the means.' A day never goes by without me fully realizing that I have had to condone the evils of greed to make sure the poor receive at least some food and the basic elements of shelter. You know the poor of Colombia do not ask for much more. At first, it seems that it cannot be correct to let the rich become richer. That may be very true, but in the end, it is their money that gives work to the poor. If I stop their excesses, I would not last long as El Presidente, and even if I did, they would not stay in Colombia; their money would go with them and more people would starve. Bill, I need your help. I cannot deliver you a drug-free economy. I was embarrassed to tell you earlier what we were doing, or rather what we were not doing. I had to say that – knowing well that you knew better. What I can say is that there is no official order to attempt to deceive. I have kept away from their discussions and I can also say that I do not personally gain from the drug industry. In less than a year, we will have the presidential elections; if I'm not elected then a candidate sympathetic to the drug industry certainly will. The drug industry will develop further, and what is more, the money will find its way out of the country to the numbered accounts of a few. The poor Colombians will not benefit.'

The two men knew he was right.

'Bill, before you speak to anybody else, please talk again to the White House and ask them to reconsider. In a few weeks, our coffee beans will be harvested and I'm told it's a good year and we must be able to sell them on the open market.'

The midday sun was providing a beautiful background to the landscape, as it does each day, making sure that the shadows were now short and strong. The pure snow-white blossom of the late-flowering coffee shrubs reflected brilliantly in the midday light. Together they walked into the shade of the bougainvillea bushes. It allowed them to continue their conversation, uninterrupted, in the pleasantly-fragrant fresh air. As they passed the edge of the water garden, they could see the droplets from the fountain bouncing and twinkling in the incident rays of the sun. They stopped simultaneously and looked at each other. El Presidente spoke. 'I need some help in my government and I know just the man. He is not a politician and currently does not live in Colombia, but he was born in Cartagena where his family still lives and where he still has considerable business connections.'

'Do I know him?'

'I don't think so. He's called, Señor Feliciano Solaccio and he owns coffee plantations, in Costa Rica and some in Colombia additionally he trades in Colombian emeralds, making jewelry for sale to the many tourists, especially the rich Americans holidaying on the Pacific coastal resorts of Mexico. His family business is in Cartagena providing many jobs in the preparation and making of jewelry for sale. I have now asked the Christian Liberal Democrats, who need a new leader, to approach him, and if he agrees I'm sure the people of Colombia would be delighted to make him their prime minister; I most certainly would. If anyone can satisfactorily sort out the problems that emanate from the drug trade, I'm sure he is just the man. He has managed to make sure the coffee cartels became properly organized to the benefit of all. He has little sympathy for the drug trade, having served three years in a British prison for smuggling drugs into England – the act of a then desperation young man. Now, only a decade later, he owns most of the market stalls in the exclusive areas on the Pacific coast of Mexico, selling expensive emerald jewelry to American tourists, and he also owns most of the coffee plantations in Costa Rica. He has more money than the drug barons and it is all legitimate and is invested in the Americas. We need him to run Colombia in the same way as he runs his own business; this would make sure that the whole world would benefit from our wonderful natural resources and we would have our coffee embargo removed forever. You see, Bill, I now have two things to do. I must persuade Feliciano Solaccio to become prime minister and then convince the White House that we are a good and reliable country. My staff are working on the first task and you are my only route to persuading the White House.

They looked at each other for seemingly a long while. El Presidente spoke. 'Let's leave it now. It is almost one o'clock. Please join me for lunch; I can see the terrace is being prepared. Cardinal Oscar will soon be arriving for our weekly lunch – he likes to speak English and doesn't often get the chance. As a young monsignor, he spent five years in London and likes very much to remember those times. Since you also have worked in London, I'm sure you will have a lot in common. Archbishop Oscar is very young to be Cardinal of Colombia, and as one of the originators of the now popular liberal theology, he is well known for his original thinking and concern for the poor people of South and Central America, and is respected in both in South America, Central America and in Europe.'

It quickly became apparent that El Presidente and the cardinal were very good friends; both, in their way, were working hard to change from the orthodoxy that restricted their respective roles. They both had very different tasks to perform and both were determined to be successful. Significantly, Pope Paul VI, Pope John Paul II, and Pope Francis have visited Colombia specially to talk directly to the people, and whilst not openly endorsing all of the cardinal's approach to liberation theology, it was interesting to note that they offered only words of encouragement. The people of Central and South America are so poor that special consideration has to be given to their needs and also to those who know them, and the Popes simply came to help.

El Presidente and the archbishop had lighter themes to consider as well as serious ones; they were both very good conversationalists and we spent the next two and a half hours in a most educationally and informatively pleasurable way. The early afternoon cooling breeze was flowing up the valley, bringing with it the natural perfumes of the countryside. Together the three of us ate well on salads and fruit and drank some of the finest wines of South America and the most aromatic of its coffee.

It was quite a surprise to find that the archbishop knew Señor Feliciano Solaccio very well. They had both been at the seminary together. When it was disbanded, the archbishop went to Rome to study and it was from there that he went to London. Was it a coincidence, thought the ambassador, that he should meet the archbishop for lunch just after El Presidente had mentioned he was seeking assistance in persuading Señor Feliciano Solaccio to become prime minister, I wonder? Did the archbishop also know that El Presidente was relying on the ambassador to get the coffee embargo lifted so that he might be given a chance to help the people of Colombia and also help the world? With both El Presidente and the Prime Minister against the drug barons, there was the possibility of some success. To change and implement new policies is always difficult and it is the one thing politicians hate to do in case they are judged as being weak, whilst it is usually anything but weakness; it is simply the opposite of that – it is an act of strength.

Paradise Island and the Cartel

The sparkling crystal chandeliers reflected the narrow shafts of light that illuminated them. Below, the Paradise Island casino was in full activity. Young mini-skirted girls were plying the punters with free drinks. The holidaymakers were enjoying this transient experience – tomorrow would they think it was worth it! More seasoned gamblers, whilst enjoying a sweet smile from the girls, refused the drink; gambling requires a very clear head. Later there would be time to enjoy a quiet meal and a drink.

Guido and his followers walked slowly through the casino. As always, they were accompanied by a bevy of young ladies – they were trying to outdo each other in their appearance. Low-cut dresses in very flimsy material struggled to cover their often-ample proportions. All of the dresses were designed to expose the maximum amount of their shapely legs; skirts were either extremely short or had slits almost to the waist. Guido stopped occasionally to acknowledge a friend or acquaintance and would sometimes pause to watch a particularly exciting game. He found the spectacle of gambling exhilarating, but it was not sufficiently stimulating for him to gamble away his own money; it was his view that there are better ways of spending it.

A smartly dressed young girl, in a very pale cream office suit, approached him, and immediately he turned and walked very purposefully to the reception area; only three of his friends accompanied him. Shaking hands with the manager, or at least with an official-looking man, they all turned and walked to the elevator.

Entering the conference room, Guido walked over to the window, his face now very serious. It was as if he had not noticed the fifteen or so men already seated at the large glass round table. One place remained empty. Looking down at the moonlit Paradise Island casino gardens, the floodlit fountains, discrete flower beds and shrubbery lights, he paused to collect his thoughts. He turned and walked to his seat. Remaining standing, he said, 'We must make sure that the government of our country does not bow to the threats of the President of the United States.' He then sat down. 'Tonight, we have all the major members of the cartels represented and we must not leave Nassau until we are all agreed on the appropriate coordinated action to take.'

A very tough-looking man was the first to speak. 'It is very simple,' he said. 'We should take the action we have always taken in the past and make it quite clear that no one should stand in our way. Why should we be concerned with the political posturing of the United States president? We make more money from cannabis, heroin, and cocaine than is made from all the coffee and emeralds put together – let's keep it that way. We have the power to push forward our requirements and we should use it so that everybody realizes what is the present situation in Colombia and how it could affect other countries. Let there are no illusions as to what is possible. Let him carry out his threat; it will not affect us. When the world sees that President of the United States is the cause of the reduction in the living standards in Colombia, he will be the one criticized.'

The tough-talking continued. Many at the Nassau meeting were from the distribution network and not from Colombia. The affairs of the Colombians were not foremost in their minds. They were, of course, concerned that their source of drugs might diminish. When it comes to drugs, the stakes are high and that makes the people involved act in a very tough manner. In the end, Guido got exactly what he wanted – all the members agreed to the use of all necessary force and each would contribute to the cost. A private mercenary army does not come cheap.

Back in Colombia and in Mexico, the production of cocaine had, if anything, been stepped up. Officially, the government was against this and had made some token efforts to destroy at least part of the production. In countries of their size, only minor official intervention was possible. More than seventy percent of production was virtually guaranteed and ninety percent likely. The government could do nothing. It would take something like the US Marines to find and destroy a significant part of the industry.

In the White House

The Secretary of State listened very carefully to what Ambassador William was saying. Dealing with foreign powers who had grown rich on American misery had always been his number one task, and that also of his foreign policy advisers. To countenance a limited flow of South American drugs into the US was a difficult ask, especially since they felt their policies were beginning to show signs of success. The ambassador wondered if he was asking for too much. The secretary of state listened and pondered, sometimes taking advice from others; he took his time. He knew El Presidente's problem was of equal importance to the US. After all, the Americas were their neighbors, especially Central America and particularly the area close to the Panama Canal, with all its commercial importance – they were all very much in their backyard. Recognising it was his responsibility to ensure their respective governments remained friends, not enemies; he was not unsympathetic to the ambassador, and eventually, after long thought, he said he was willing to recommend to the United States president that the coffee embargo be delayed, but at the same time he was at great pains to point out there had not been a change of policy; the flow of drugs must slow and eventually cease. Before the president was approached, it was necessary to get some agreement from other departments, in particular, the CIA and the FBI. With both of them in the front line in the fight against drugs, their acquiescence was not going to be easy.

Later that day, the President of the United States listened patiently and carefully to the arguments presented. He made little comment and only rarely asked for clarification. The Secretary of State had put forward a sound case for postponing the coffee embargo, but it was the ever-present threat that communism might establish itself close to the southern boundary of the US that influenced him most, reliable stable governments in the Americas were most important. The President agreed to delay the embargo for twelve months, with a review to take place immediately following the Colombian elections. The directors of the CIA and FBI, particularly the FBI, were not happy, but recognized the threat that could come from their neighbors had to be considered.

The Colombian coffee harvest was now secure, meaning El Presidente would certainly now have a good chance of winning the election. The immediate task was now to convince Señor Feliciano Solaccio to run with him as prime minister.

Bogotá

The US ambassador immediately flew back to Bogotá. He was still not certain his student friend, El Presidente, was secure; even though the US was going to support him in a very practical and positive way. As the plane touched down, he started to feel apprehensive. Political life in South America is never very easy and the solution to one problem often simply means that you just move on to the next one – the list is never-ending.

He was met at the airport diplomatic exit by James, the First Secretary, and his chauffeur.

'I see your flight was on time; I trust it was comfortable.'

'Yes, it was very comfortable and I'm fresh and ready for business. Shall I ring El Presidente from the car?'

Courteously, he replied, 'I think it's better if you go to see him personally. El Presidente will be ready to see you, I am sure.'

The drive to the presidential palace was about fifty-five minutes – at first through the outskirts of the city and then into the hills. It was now early in the evening, the end of a very hot day and the drive into the mountains was dramatically lovely. The aroma of the oleander and bougainvillea perfumes mixed with the wild mountain herbs, together with the aromatic smell of burning wood was invigorating – it was a wonderful experience.

The gates of the residence opened automatically and the car sped through. By the time they stopped in the courtyard, El Presidente was already waiting for them. The First Secretary stood well back as the two friends greeted each other warmly. Immediately, El Presidente spoke. 'Bill, are you bringing good news?' Turning slowly, they walked down to the sunken gardens where they would not be overheard. El Presidente broke the short silence. 'I can see from your face, Bill, that you have good news. I knew I could rely on you. Will your country help us?'

'Well, we will do our best. The President of the United States has ordered the coffee embargo to be postponed for twelve months, certainly until after the elections. However, I must warn you that it might be changed and it will depend very much on the outcome of the elections.'

'Thank you, Bill, and thank your president for his help. I know it has not been easy and I appreciate our drugs cause real misery to some of your countrymen. We need your help and God will reward you, of that I'm sure, and together we will make Colombia a peaceful neighbor and a neighbor you can trust and rely on.'

'Well, El Presidente, have you made progress with your running mate?'

'Yes, my advisor, the general secretary of the CDP, Jacinta, met him whilst she was in Cartagena. We're still waiting for his agreement. Tomorrow, the cardinal is in Cartagena and he will also speak to him. Señor Feliciano Solaccio is a good man, and although he has citizenship in

Mexico, Costa Rica, as well as Colombia, he remains true to his family roots and is a firm Colombian. So far, few know of our plans – to release information would give our opponents time to counter and that could be dangerous.'

Down through the gardens, they walked; the large gardens made sure they were alone. Following at a discreet distance was the First Secretary and two of El Presidente's staff. By the fountain, they stopped to admire the flood-lit water jets and the lively sparkling droplets. A few moments later, a butler appeared with the drinks trolley.

'May I offer you a margarita? They are just right at this time in the evening and I hope you will be able to stay and have dinner with us. Tonight, we are dining by the fountain.' Alfresco dining is very popular as the heat of the day cools into the warmth of the evening.

The ambassador would have preferred to go home, but he didn't have the heart to say no. The First Secretary tactfully declined the invitation and returned to his flat in one of the presidential cars.

About half an hour and several margaritas later, the Colombian First Lady appeared. She walked slowly towards them, accompanied by a much younger lady. Both were coolly dressed in pastel green and blue respectively, their diaphanous dresses fluttering in the gentle breeze. Although of different ages, they were dressed similarly. Both had gleaming jet-black hair pulled back tightly from the face. The ambassador had met the First Lady many times before, but he did not immediately recognize the young lady. He stepped forward to greet them.

'Mr. Ambassador, how good of you to come immediately to see my husband, and I can see from your smile you have brought good news. Allow me to introduce Jacinta, a member of my husband's staff; then I'm sure you already know her.'

'Madam Eleanor, I am very pleased to be here and, yes, I do know Miss Mendez. What a beautiful time of the year and how delightful is your garden and how wonderful is the evening atmosphere – it's a lovely time to be outside.'

'It certainly is and what could be better than to have dinner out in the open; I believe dinner is almost ready,' said Eleanor.

Turning to her husband, El Presidente, she said, 'The temperature is just right for us to dine out on the terrace.'

Linking arms with the ambassador, they walked across the lawn and up the steps. El Presidente followed on with Jacinta; on an informal evening such as this, the protocol of El Presidente walking first was dropped.

Eleanor dominated the conversation at dinner. Turning to Jacinta, she said, 'This evening, the men are not going to be given the chance to talk shop – as ex-Harvard students, El Presidente and William have a lot in common. If we give them half a chance, they would either be talking politics or reminiscing about times past. It's my experience that men tend to talk much more than women! Mr. Ambassador, it's a pity your wife is not also here this evening – she will be wondering where you are.'

'I spoke to her from the plane, so she knows where I am; I just wanted to talk to El Presidente about my trip to Washington.

'Yes, I understand, and I can see you have brought good news. Colombia needs friends and with you, Mr. Ambassador, we are very lucky.'

'Madam Eleanor, I have spent many years in Colombia, and Cartagena is one of my favorite cities. The autumn is such a delightful time and when the heat of the day has gone and fresh flowers are beginning to bloom it is lovely. Many times, El Presidente and I have spent the evening together, talking until the small hours, drinking wine or beer or coffee or even all three.'

'You are quite right you know, William, on an evening such as this, I am pleased to be living in the palace. It is not often that life is proceeding in the way you want and it always embarrasses me to think that we have so much, yet the ordinary Colombians have so little. I pray daily that God will help and I do think that we will succeed. I was down at the clinic this morning. The new babies looked wonderful and the sisters were helping the young mothers – teaching them how to look after them. The girls look so young and the babies looked wonderfully healthy. The climate of Colombia is one of the best in the world and it can give protection to all.'

'Well, there's a lot to be done, that's for sure, and somebody has to do it.'

'We certainly won't be able to solve our problems tonight.' Looking towards El Presidente, she remarked, 'I can see he is happy and his confidence is beginning to return.'

Jacinta turned to the ambassador. 'You have traveled throughout Colombia I understand.'

'Yes, well many of the cities and some of the accessible countryside, but I have spent most of my time in Bogotá and Cartagena. I must say as the First Lady implied Cartagena is my first love. The old city, the market, the cafés, and the cooling sea breeze.'

'When did you first visit Colombia?'

'Oh, it's a long time ago – I think I was still at Harvard. I was interested in botany and I think it was on my first field study visit that my interest in the politics of the Americas was conceived. I completed my first degree in botany and then stayed on to do a master's in political law. The disciplines were so different. I needed to do a further four years of study. During the vacations, I would often visit Colombia. Later, I entered the diplomatic service, and I was pleased to be placed in the South and Central American department and spent most of my time in Colombia with a little time in Brazil. I think Cartagena is my real home; we have a villa on the coast and go there very often, whenever the opportunity occurs.'

'Do you also have a home in the US?'

'No, not now. We used it so little. Now, when we go back, we rent an apartment. There is a possibility I might buy a condominium in Florida so that I don't become completely Colombianized.' He smiled rather unconvincingly.

'I think Bill's interest in the Colombian people and coffee will always override his US citizenship,' smiled El Presidente. 'Although I know once an American, always an American, but you must have spent more of your time south of the equator then north of it. I think, Eleanor, he now looks as Spanish as we do, and certainly, he can truthfully claim to speak our language fluently and better than many.'

'That is certainly so,' she replied. 'And your wife, I understand she has ties to this country. Are they as strong as yours?'

'Yes, I must say she always looks happy and content here. Her family comes from Central America, from Panama and Costa Rica, so she is very much at home. Our children are back in the States and will stay there, I think.'

'Are they also diplomats?'

'No, my daughter is a surgeon as also is one of my sons.

The other is a computer engineer and they all live in and around the San Francisco area. Jacinta, do you know San Francisco?'

'Yes, I know San Francisco. It is an attractive city, and a few years ago I also spent some time at the Berkeley campus of the University of California. It also was very interesting; in parts, it is a bit like Colombia and I liked it very much.'

'What were you doing at Berkeley?'

'I was teaching South and Central American history at the university and at the same time learning about the American way of life.'

'What did you think of it?'

'It certainly is very different; I like it very much. Certainly, it's a land of plenty, but sadly not for everybody.'

'San Francisco is noted for its liberal free life.' He was taking care not to mention the well-known problem of drugs and homelessness. Tonight, was a time for happy conversation, not to illustrate the problems encountered in some parts of the United States.

'I think it is one of the few places where a perfect blend of people exists. Sadly, that is not true in most of the great cities of the world.'

'In Colombia, we do not have many visiting families or new immigrants – it's far too poor for that. Almost all our citizens are Colombians or people from close or near Central America.

I remember once taking the ferry from Fisherman's Wharf to Sausalito. It was then that I realized why the US is rich and why Colombia is poor. It was a very bright clear morning and as we pulled away from the jetty, I could see the sun shining on the magnificence of the Bay Bridge over which I had just traveled from Berkeley. As we passed close to Alcatraz Island, the magnificence of the Golden Gate Bridge could now be seen through the lifting sea fog. These bridges were built during the depression years and at a time of little or no confidence – a time when there was a real loss of spirit in the USA. Fortunately, the spirit of Franklin D Roosevelt did not waiver; he saw that it was the time to put America to work and, in doing so, provide the infrastructure for a great future economy that would make America a strong nation again. The bridges are not simply edifices; they are large practical investments, some two-tiered, designed to carry the ever-increasing traffic as future wealth was created. This entrepreneurial approach was required back then, as it is now in Colombia. We want our government to build the equivalent of the Golden Gate and Bay Bridges to give work to our people and to create a sound economic bridge to our future.'

The table was silent as Jacinta spoke. I suppose they were thinking about what Colombia's future would be like. It is a resource-rich country, rich in energy, rich in land and populated by people wanting to work and waiting to be led into work.

Time was now getting on and it had been a long day for all, especially for the ambassador. It was time for him to return home. Jacinta sent for the chauffeur and soon he had gone. She then drove home.

Nassau Again

Whilst the US Ambassador was with El Presidente in Bogotá, in Nassau, the Medellin 'executive' was considering the US threat to boycott, not only coffee but pretty much the whole of Colombian overseas trade; such a boycott would have serious effects on all its agricultural and mineral exports.

At this stage, the US threat to boycott Colombian coffee was not judged by the cartels to be that important, even though it did illustrate how the US, by its actions, could affect the whole economy of any part of the Americas. The price of coffee on the international market had increased on the rumor. To some, this might be good. Inca Inc. (Costa Rica) was making increased profits, and with its storage system, the previous years' beans were also increasing in value. They were starting to supply both the US and Europe. Jamaican Blue Mountain Arabica beans had hit an all-time high, not only on the American markets, but throughout the world. At this stage, the threat was mainly affecting the coffee growers and their cartels; other trade would soon be affected.

A boycott could have a considerable effect on all the cartels' activities, although today their major problem was not the illegality of their drug trade, for they were all devoid of conscience and had only one main goal in life and that was making money. Now, it was the handling of its finances. The growth of drugs and their preparation essentially looked after itself. A far bigger problem was presenting itself and one that was not so easy to solve. Enormous amounts of cash were now being generated and it was beginning to be extremely difficult to deal with it. It was mainly because the money received from drug sales was in relatively small denominations, and therefore, it was difficult to move into existing financial systems without it being obvious that it might be coming from an illegal source – banks and other financial institutions were wary of handling it, doing so would then put them on the wrong side of the law. Such large quantities of small denomination cash do not readily occur in modern commercial systems, except perhaps in retail. It was a constant problem as to how they could manage the complicated flow of money, from the drug sales, back to the drug barons in Colombia. A system was required to legalize the money, but how?

In the early days, the casinos and their associated so-called gambling organizations could convert all the cash they had into their legal bank accounts. The cleaned money could then be used or transferred through the international markets with impunity. After all, gambling, by its very nature, is a vehicle for cash movement, and no country giving a license to a casino could be fussy about the origin of the money circulating within it. The situation was now becoming very different. With such huge amounts of money involved, larger conversion facilities were required. Even Feliciano Solaccio's original Soviet system was now overwhelmed.

With this in mind, it was not surprising that money laundering was the main item on today's agenda; the

Colombian presidential election was secondary. The US threat to boycott Colombian coffee was important but not that important. It was, however, realized that if the American threat could have such an immediate influence on the international market price of coffee, causing it to increase almost overnight, it indicated how the American government could influence the world economy in all sorts of ways and the plight of Colombia might, in some way, also directly affect them. Currently, they were making plenty of money; that was all well and good and they wanted it to continue.

The objective of tonight's meeting was to consider plans for the future. Initially, they knew nothing of the recent developments with the United States; they did not know about the lifting of the Colombian coffee embargo by the US president. It was not until later in the evening when Alfredo, the Colombian finance minister, arrived, that the meeting first heard of the US coffee reprieve and what its consequences might be. Loans would now be made by the G7 governments to the Colombian government to allow them to develop their countries economy and in so doing make it less dependent on the dark drug trade. The International Monetary Fund would play an important part in planning for the future; considerable funds would be available to finance Colombia's extensive infrastructure and its new utility supply systems, together with the advance of social services, health and education. The meeting suddenly came to life when they realized that over the next ten years, there was upwards of several hundred billion dollars to be spent; providing them with the possibility that these funds could be used in some way to launder their vast amounts of drug money. Large international contracts would be involved and it was within these contracts that possible advantages to them could be found.

Alfredo reminded them that, with inside civil service help, most of that could be used in an elaborate switching process, converting their tainted drug profits into clean International Monetary Fund money.

As minister for finance, he was currently able to have some influence on the placing of all these new contracts. Inevitably, the contracts would go to foreign companies mainly in the United States and Europe, and the financial arrangements would be through international banks. 'It is important,' he said, 'that I remain in my position of Colombian finance minister. Next spring is the presidential election, and that is when we could have problems. We must make sure that problems do not occur.'

'If El Presidente is re-elected,' said Alfredo, 'then the IMF loan is secure. All we need now is a sympathetic prime minister and our schemes will be okay.'

'There lies the problem,' continued Alfredo. 'We know that El Presidente has been seeing the US ambassador recently and also Jacinta has been meeting Señor Feliciano Solaccio. El Presidente must be planning something for the future and I am not at all sure that I will be part of it. I've tried to get information from Stephanie. So far, it's been unsuccessful – her father is giving nothing away. El Presidente maybe my father-in-law, but what exactly my position in his plans will be I do not know. I'm not at all certain I will be in my present position after the election. My present privileged position of finance minister may go to a less sympathetic candidate.'

Back in Bogotá

The presidential election was now only two weeks away and El Presidente seemed all set for a further five years in office. However, the government to support him was not so secure. Alfredo was not at all confident of his future and he was now planning an action strategy for his survival.

High in the mountains, remote from the press, he met his friends. So remote was it, 4x4 vehicles were required to get there, and to ensure that they were not seen together, four vehicles had travelled on separate days to avoid the risk of exposure. Alfredo travelled last.

He was driven by a young lady driver, smart in her fine fawn uniform. She was dark and her eyes shone like stars. Her use of make-up highlighted her pretty face and the shine of her hair and sparkle of her very brown eyes made her a picture. Alfredo wondered how a very young girl could handle such a powerful machine.

Through the woodlands, they travelled, first on semi-metalized roads then onto tracks often made uneven by the mountain rains. How she navigated he could not tell; occasionally she would turn onto a track that, to him, looked exactly like others – how she knew it was the correct one was a mystery. After about two hours, the forest started to fall away and the land opened up, exposing the beauty of the area. The richness of the woodland had now gone, and the terrain took on a vista, not unlike parts of the Middle East. No longer subject to the tropical rains of the forest, the ground was stony, consisting of limestone and sandstone with occasional clumps of shrub. After a while, what little fauna there was, disappeared, and alpine-like mountains reached to the sky. Then they had arrived at a mountain lodge tucked into the rocks.

Marietta jumped down from the truck, quickly adjusting her skirt. She hurried around to open the door for Alfredo and supervised the removal of his briefcase from the back. Several men appeared from the lodge to help her.

Inside the wooden cabin, all was ready for the meeting. Alfredo was the last to arrive and wished to stay the minimum possible amount of time. The three men and one woman looked very serious as he explained that if the election pole analysis in the press was correct, El Presidente's re-election was likely and the government was going to change to a more centralized democratic legislature, led by a new prime minister, possibly Señor Feliciano Solaccio. The days of bribing the electorate were over. Satellite TV had seen to that. CNN News from the US was received by many of the electorate, neutralizing any prejudicial domestic propaganda. The new administration was offering much, and the possible IMF loan would guarantee these offers. US support was seen, by many, to make the loan guarantee copper-bottomed. We are just going to have to accept a new political regime. Not all was bad for them; a new opportunity was opening up. They could benefit by using the IMF financed contracts to launder the ever-increasing problem of the vast amounts of 'contaminated' drug money. They spent the next two days planning such schemes.

The New Prime Minister

Feliciano had been up for more than two hours, and at 6:45 he walked through the old city down to the shore where he strolled, as he often did, along the water's edge. It would be nearly a further hour before the sun would rise and the heat of a new autumn day would bless the start of the harvesting season where the workers would painstakingly collect the coffee beans. The temperature, around the sixties, was just right for a morning stroll, and for some time, Feliciano walked slowly, then quickly, sometimes stopping to gaze out to sea. The gentle breeze was just perfect and pleasantly perfumed with the plantation fragrances from a bountiful region. Eventually, he returned to his room at the Imperial Hotel in the old city of Cartagena just in time to answer the ringing telephone.

'I'm in the lobby.' He recognized Jacinta's voice. 'May I join you for breakfast?'

Feliciano's heart missed a beat, not because it was Jacinta, although that would make most men's heart flicker a little. No – he realized that she was here for a serious discussion. He had thought of little else over the last few days since their first meeting and he was no nearer to a decision.

A few minutes later, they met in the lounge and together they entered the restaurant. Only a very small number of people were already breakfasting; breakfast is not the most popular meal of the day with the late-night Carthaginians' and their guests. Feliciano was quite hungry and ordered a typical American breakfast of pancakes, crispy bacon, eggs, and syrup, followed by fresh fruit and, of course, accompanied by Colombian coffee. Jacinta was satisfied with croissants and coffee.

For a while, they spoke about life generally. Feliciano did not initially realize that Jacinta had only just arrived from Bogotá for this meeting; her fresh appearance belied the fact that she really must be very tired after traveling most of the night. Jacinta was not going to waste too much time, and soon she was down to business. She spoke very quietly and rattled her cutlery to mask what she was saying – hidden eavesdropping microphones could be anywhere. 'Please, Señor Solaccio, before you say anything about our meeting on Sunday, may I say that there have been developments.' Feliciano knew exactly what was coming. 'El Presidente,' she added, 'wants me to tell you that the US president has relented on the coffee embargo, but it is conditional on you accepting the post of prime minister.'

Jacinta had now seen Señor Feliciano Solaccio on only one earlier occasion, and with the government unlikely to last much longer, she was now applying pressure on him. In the end, his decision to allow his name to go forward as a candidate to be prime minister was made easy. She described how the cartels had moved to stop her party by attacking their city office, injuring fifteen of the staff. Jacinta was safe; she had a government bodyguard, although that was not in itself a guarantee, for she had been personally attacked on no less than four occasions. If she and her colleagues were prepared to take such risks, thought Feliciano, then he was prepared to help. For a while, they were both silent. Feliciano carried on eating as if nothing had happened. He was quiet for more than twenty minutes, and then simply nodded in acceptance. 'Thank god,' she smiled in reply.

The Political Picture in Colombia

The political hierarchy of Colombia now had a new face – one very few people had seen before. Señor Feliciano Solaccio was completely unknown outside the emerald beach market and the Costa Rican coffee industries. His name came as a surprise to everybody; they had no idea why El Presidente had selected an unknown to run with him as his prime minister. Needless to say, they very quickly started to check his background and it wasn't long before his successes as a beach trader in emeralds and later as a coffee grower were known to everybody. Interestingly and more important, was that his reputation was presented positively and attractively. Many people were prepared to give witness to how well he had looked after them and how he made sure that they were all well-paid and that all the profits of his companies remained in the countries where they were made: Colombia, Mexico and Costa Rica.

The drug cartel was taken by surprise. They were left with little time to work out a new strategy. Should they attack Señor Feliciano Solaccio's recent blemish-free record or should they simply try to stop him being voted for, using whatever means they could? It came as a considerable surprise to all when they realized that he once played an important part in the drug export trade, and was largely responsible for developing the European market and, much more importantly, played a very important part in developing a safe and secure money-laundering system; a scheme making sure that all the profits in the drug business returned home to Colombia. Even in those days, he had a reputation for trying to look after the Colombian economy. He did not want offshore banks benefiting from the drug baron's money. Although this was a long time ago, he still had friends in the drug trade. His reputation remained high; he was the sort of person who recognized all his workers and tried hard to treat them all the same, and consequently, he remained friendly with all of them and was very well respected. It wasn't long before the history of his emerald beach market trading organization and his involvement in the coffee growing in Costa Rica was known. Perhaps what was more disturbing to the drug cartel was how he and Maria Guadalupe had rendered the coffee cartel members ineffective – their members moving to agree with Feliciano Solaccio and Maria Guadalupe. The growers had realized the system they had was unsatisfactory and that a real commercial approach was the way to bring profits to all. Unfortunately, many of the coffee growers were indecisive and moved only slowly away from the cartels. They were forced to sell their plantations, usually to Inca Inc. (Costa Rica). Feliciano and Maria Guadalupe Solaccio took no commercial advantage of this; they bought their plantations at realistic prices satisfying the owners, many of whom were quite happy to move away from the domineering cartel restraints.

It quickly became apparent to the drug cartel members that El Presidente had been shrewd and careful in the selection of his new prime minister-elect. No matter what they did now, they were going to be in trouble, especially if they used fear to make the people vote against him. In any event, that was not practical and would be extremely difficult. More likely it would make them vote for El Presidente and his prime minister.

Alfredo was having to accept that his family connection to El Presidente was unlikely to help him anymore; he was now destined to become a weak member of both the government and the cartel.

The Election

With the elections for a new president and government now only a few weeks away, life in the presidential palace was tense. The US would probably lose confidence in them if El Presidente, together with his new prime minister, were not elected. Should they not be returned, it could mean the loan could be in jeopardy.

In due course, the election took place with very little interference from the cartels, and El Presidente and Señor Feliciano Solaccio were elected. Both were returned with large majorities; the people of Colombia had made their choice and they were all seemed very happy with the result.

It was now up to El Presidente and Señor Feliciano Solaccio to deliver a government that was acceptable to all – a formidable task. It was never going to be easy governing a large country whilst, at the same time, juggling with two opposing powers – the United States of America and the internal drug cartels. Nevertheless, it was necessary for some kind of amicable agreement to be reached. It had to be accepted that it was not possible to get rid of the drug cartels now or soon, but one thing was important and that was Colombian drugs must not enter the United States. How to do this was not at all clear. Fortunately, the current interest of the drug cartels was more in laundering money than selling drugs; whilst there were users, supplying them was relatively simple – it was happening anyway.

As expected, Alfredo was no longer in a principal position within the government. Nevertheless, his time in government had made him aware that the first step to improving the country's economy would be to quickly develop its infrastructure, allowing the economy to expand, and so benefit all with good education, medical care and general welfare. The United States was very much on the side of El Presidente and was instrumental in ensuring the IMF provided the loans from which his plans could be accomplished. Alfredo was hoping that this presented an opportunity to help the cartels with their money laundering problems and further it was likely that it would go unnoticed by the prime minister and El Presidente – at least at first. Whilst in government, he had planned the ways the IMF money might help them. Now his efforts were fully directed to using the contract-based movement of money to 'clean' the cartels' profit.

After the Election

For a while, the IMF loan was held up by the G7 governments. Some thought that the internal affairs of Colombia were their problem and were not internationally important. The World Security Forces meeting in Rio thought differently. They confirmed that the fight with the drug barons was international and would not be won by the simple expedient of making it illegal or by the economic tool of restricting trade with the countries exporting drugs – something more radical was necessary. All accepted that a new plan was essential and any plan certainly needed the help of the US president. As far as Colombia was concerned, economic help was required and the purchase of their coffee was essential. All the South and Central American Nations were now working together, supporting legitimate commerce. The plan was simple enough – build an economy that did not need drugs or the drug barons. Then together, their new healthy economies would drive the drug industry away, not just move it underground.

The development of countries like Colombia required immediate financial help, with IMF help, and with their supervision, they would ensure the avoidance of ecological damage frequently found in South America developments.

Immediately after the Rio meeting, the British prime minister visited Cartagena to reassure the El Presidente and prime minister that the IMF would help develop their economy in a way that still allowed Colombia and the whole world to benefit from one of their valuable assets – the rainforests. We all know they are important in providing natural oxygen to the atmosphere. The trees are perfect custodians of the atmosphere and the environment, soaking up carbon dioxide and breathing out pure fresh oxygen; nature knows best how to look after itself and after us. De-forestation not only prevents oxygen production, but it also re-releases previously trapped carbon dioxide from newly exposed land. The rain forests must not be touched.

Before the final decision on the IMF loan could be made, it was necessary for the countries involved to know exactly the extent of the work and the total cost.

The respectable Swiss International Construction Company had been chosen by the IMF to make preliminary studies on the scope of the project. This well-known and reliable company may then become responsible for the whole of the project. Petra Pirrein was in overall charge. The supervisory contract would be the largest the company had ever known and Petra had been given carte blanche to secure it if possible. Swiss International Construction might be about to receive the largest contract ever awarded to a single company. The International Monetary Fund was likely to agree to make upwards of $200 billion available to the Colombian government. In return, it expected a stable country which would develop legitimate trade. The US president had approved it all; to him, the drugs problem was now so serious, nothing less than this ambitious plan was required.

The first step was to provide a complete road network, fully integrated with air and sea international links. Agricultural development would then follow and power systems installed. Modern communications, education and healthcare were to be set up. Above all, the real treasures of the country were to be preserved. The rainforests of Colombia would remain and continue to feedback life-supporting oxygen.

The US president's plan was underway and it was now the task to finally choose the individual contractors acceptable to the IMF and the Colombian government.

In the morning, Petra was first briefed on how El Presidente would like things to go. She might even meet him. Señorita Jacinta would be her contact – how young she looked, was Petra's first impression. 'Welcome to Colombia, Señora Pirrein. El Presidente wishes me to help you in any way I can. Colombia is waiting to move forward into the next millennium. We are a country whose riches are dormant and whose people are patiently waiting for politicians and economists to help them. I know that well – my parents worked hard all their lives and have little to show.' She blushed a little as Petra said, without thinking, 'I'm sure they are very proud of you.'

'Later, we will meet the new finance minister and his colleagues in the treasury and the interior. They will handle the day to day running of any contract. First, let me tell you about our president and prime minister; I am sure you have heard of both of them – men of great integrity.'

For the next hour or so, Jacinta spoke about the successful results of the presidential elections. She was frank, political life in any country cannot be taken for granted, least of all in

South and Central America. She explained how the lifelong friendship between the US ambassador and El Presidente had been crucial and that now it was necessary to bring about the changes required for Colombia and the rest of the world.

This was a curious phrase, thought Petra – changes necessary for Colombia and the rest of the world – what did that mean? Jacinta paused for a while as she spoke. An explanation did not come and Petra felt she should not ask. Nevertheless, the phrase stayed in her mind.

Jacinta continued, 'Colombia has been having difficulties over the past decade or so – that is certainly well known. It is the same problem for all the Americas, south of the Californian-Mexican-Florida parallel. They are all very rich in natural resources and people, but they are all poorly developed. The successful ideologies of Western Europe have now incited some citizens to ask for similar equality. The wealth of North America has not gone unnoticed. The political and economic stability of new central and South American governments has not been easy. I'm sure you will remember the promising start in Brazil a few decades ago, sadly it did not ripen to fulfillment.

'In Colombia, we have a president who has the confidence of most of the people; that is rare. We now have Señor Feliciano Solaccio as our new prime minister – I have arranged for you to meet him. El Presidente is popular; we do not doubt that, and we are sure his new prime minister will be just as popular. He is not well known outside this area.

'Medellin is one of our problems. They have been since the 40s, but not everything is bad about Medellin. They look after a large part of the country where there is now good health care, social care and education. However, it is not democratically controlled, and, of course, it is not good to build an economy based on the directions of a few. Now a lot depends on you and the IMF contract and the effect it will have.'

'But I do not have the contract,' said Petra, 'I am here to negotiate it and contracts like this are not easily won.'

'Yes, I can appreciate that and I have no power to give it to you – neither does El Presidente. Some presidents in South America have absolute power and exercise it; not El Presidente. He is responsible for the government; the cabinet will confirm any decision. You must know that we have two economies in Colombia. One is transparent and open: coffee, energy, gold and emeralds; the other is opaque and murky but just as powerful – only it is limited to a few. We export a product that is not welcomed by all and efforts are being made to stop it. We can expect that one-day they will be successful, but today, Colombia has nothing to replace it – well, not at the moment. So, you can see there are very good reasons for driving our president to bring about changes. We want all our people to have a reasonably prosperous life based on good ethical and legitimate trade. A lifetime of effort has gone into this dream; now, with the help of the US President, we are beginning to awake to a morning of optimism – so much depends on this, possibly it's our only chance.'

Later that day Petra met Señor Jair, the Colombian finance minister, they had met before in Switzerland. He had seen the original plans for the trunk road interconnecting highway system that would take Colombia into the twenty-first century. The Swiss International Construction Company had spent a year working on the details. A complete scale model of Colombia was on display in the center of the exhibition room in the Sheraton hotel in Zürich. The proposed highway system was highlighted with day-glow lines, some of which penetrated deep into the rainforest. The plan was to make the whole of Colombia accessible, and yet still retain the ecology of the country.

This afternoon, Señor Jair was both elegant and effective – and we got down to business quickly. 'We have,' he said, 'the target of finalizing the contract before the weekend. Any delay would mean that it might be referred back to the IMF in New York and the outcome could then be uncertain. The interior ministry is satisfied that you can handle the entire project and we are pleased with the preparations that have already been made. A company that is prepared to spend its own money to make sure that work starts on time and to ensure it is managed well is a company we are pleased to work with. Together we must now check the document of intent so that it can be signed on Sunday in the presidential palace.'

Our meeting had lasted only about thirty minutes and I could see my mission to Colombia was essentially complete. The two IMF officials agreed to the Colombian development plan. Takia Sumati from Japan and Sergio Collumbini from Italy would supervise the task and effectively make the final decisions. The selection of the sub-contractors would then follow and Swiss International Construction would supervise the detailed planning. They had prepared the initial scheme and understood all its detail well. Their construction cost was more reliable than that of other competitors, a point of great concern to the IMF, costly overruns can be most embarrassing to them and can lead to late modification of their plans and still worse cancellations.

It was hoped that the work would start soon, at an

estimated cost of $200 billion over ten years. Equating approximately $20 billion each year, this would be the largest-ever contract given on any commercial scheme and certainly by the IMF; it was greater than some of the large US defense and space contracts of the 60s and the 70s.

After the IMF council have rubber-stamped the scheme; tendering would start immediately. Although costs would play an important part, in the end, it would most likely go to the companies that were acceptable to Colombia.

They had a further two days of meetings, checking the fine detail. Petra now thought she would now be home for Christmas – well just.

Signing the contract was a simple, but very formal occasion. It was signed in the presence of El Presidente and his wife, the retired and the new prime ministers, Señorita Jacinta, and the ambassadors of the UK and US and Petra. Surprisingly, neither the finance nor the interior ministers were present. The US ambassador was the representative of the IMF. All the signed documents would be kept at the presidential palace; only copies would be available back in New York and London.

As Petra signed the document she nervously wondered if the flourish of her normal signature was possible. Picking up the malachite fountain pen, she could feel her muscles tense, would she be able to write at all. After the signing, El Presidente presented Petra with the pen; later Señorita Jacinta gave her an inscribed presentation leather case to keep it in. Lunch on the terrace was a simple yet splendid meal of fruit and fish with light white wine and Colombian coffee to follow.

Petra now fully realized why Señor Feliciano Solaccio was their new prime minister. He was young and not a politician by desire; a true Colombian with a real interest in its people and their prosperity and as an immensely rich man in his own right he fully realized the necessity of using the money for the benefit of others. His workers had benefited from this and so did he. He was a bachelor. She wondered if Señorita Jacinta was more than an admirer of him. She was fond of both El Presidente and Señor Feliciano Solaccio and for the former, it was the love of a daughter.

Los Angeles

With so much depending on help from the President of the United States of America, both El Presidente and the Colombian prime minister needed to remain in close contact with him. Any possible chance of inadvertent misunderstanding must be avoided at all costs. Important decisions were now being made and both presidents thought direct contact was necessary. So far, they had only spoken on the telephone; even so, there was no doubt they all got on very well. South American presidents rarely leave their countries' and it was very unlikely that the United States president would visit Colombia. There was the possibility that the United States president and the Colombian prime minister might meet at some time in the United States. No special moves were made; however, an opportunity presented itself when the US president planned a visit to Los Angeles. Recognizing a meeting might be possible, the Secretary of State contacted their ambassador in Bogotá, asking if Señor Feliciano Solaccio could visit Los Angeles. If this was possible then an informal meeting between them could be arranged.

Señor Feliciano Solaccio and Jacinta arrived in Los Angeles

two days before the president for preliminary talks with the Secretary of State. Now he was ready to meet the US president as soon as he arrived. They met at the US Consulate.

Rather interestingly, their conversation was, in the main, general. Of course, the president knew about Señor Feliciano Solaccio's past. However, today he was far more interested in the present. He wanted to know more about the man he was to rely on for help in reducing the flow of drugs into the United States and indeed out to the rest of the world. Both men were aware that while producers and users want drugs, their trade would continue. The problem was going to be extremely difficult to solve; indeed, a solution might well be impossible. With the redevelopment of the economies of countries like Colombia, there might just be a chance of reducing reliance on this evil problem. For this to happen, it was mainly up to local political leaders, and in particular, men like the Colombian prime minister. Was he the right man to make the first positive moves? The president wanted to personally see if Señor Feliciano Solaccio was up to it – did he have a safe pair of hands. Essentially, he wanted to judge for himself if Ambassador William's assessment was correct.

The meeting came as a surprise to Jacinta and she was intrigued that such a discussion was even possible, although she was aware of the US president's informal approach to ensuring success from all those around him. He was well known for his very careful approach to the running of the world's most powerful economy, and he fully realized how important it was to have the correct men working with him. Jacinta also realized that before the IMF agreed to the much-needed financial help for Colombia, it required full US presidential approval; the US was not just simply buying

Colombia's coffee!

The discussions lasted for nearly two hours – a very long time for the president to spend with a single person. As expected, the president was particularly interested in the prime minister's experience with the coffee cartels, and how he was successful in convincing its members that freedom of trade had attractions with real benefits. Also, how he had shown them that there was much more to be gained from individual free trade then there was in being too tightly tied to each other. He was interested in every aspect of what had happened in Costa Rica, and particularly how Maria Guadalupe had successfully fought off the physical attempts trying to intimidate her into abandoning her management of the plantations. He was so interested that he said he would like to meet Maria Guadalupe and further asked if it was possible for her to visits Los Angeles before he went home. Maria Guadalupe was only too pleased to oblige and was able to get the next plane from Mexico to Los Angeles; they would be able to meet in the morning.

Time was now getting on and an anxious secretary whispered to the president that he was already behind schedule and that the state governors were patiently waiting.

Dominique

Around 2:30 p.m., the First Lady arrived for the evening's entertainment. She knew Jacinta well and they chatted enthusiastically. She was more than happy to look after us for the rest of the afternoon, and she invited us to have English afternoon tea at the consulate before going on to the ballet in the evening. Being a knowledgeable ballet enthusiast and a friend of the Russian prima ballerina Anneliese Linden, she was also looking forward to the evening's performance of Swan Lake. Los Angeles was the last stop in the Bolshoi Company's tour of the US.

For me, the evening was difficult to describe – it was simply marvelous. It was the first time I had seen a live ballet performance and I did not know what to expect. Certainly, I did not think it would be anywhere near as spectacular as it was; the music, the costumes and above all the dancing were exquisite.

Attending a ballet performance was something very new to me. I was unfamiliar with the story and knew little of what it would be like. Fortunately, the First Lady had prepared us for the spectacle. Swan Lake, like many ballets, is a mixture of romance, tragedy and magic. Sorcerers usually play an important part in every fairy tale tragedy. Odette, under the sorcerer's spell, spends her days as a swan swimming on a lake of tears, returning at night to her wonderful and beautiful human form. Swan Lake is a little unusual in that the principal dancer usually plays the duel part of Odette, the beautiful feminine dancer, and Odile, the hard-headed sorcerer's daughter. As with all fairy tales the plot is complex, but as also with all fairytales, there is a happy ending with Odette and Prince Siegfried dancing off into the future, with the swans of the *corps de ballet* guiding them into the heavens above the lake.

The musical and visual response required no preparation. As one would expect, the music was just wonderful; how anyone could compose such evocative sounds is beyond my comprehension. I certainly do not understand the process in which the music is first composed and then how the delicate dancing is choreographed into the story. For me, I would have been happy to simply close my eyes and listen to the music; only then I would be missing the main part of the ballet – the magnificence of the dancing. My first impression was how beautiful the dancers looked; although it's quite clear that the make-up and hairstyling had very much changed their natural appearance, nevertheless, I was near enough to see their faces and how strikingly young they were. I could also see the beads of perspiration on their foreheads and the heartbeat of their breasts as they exerted an enormous amount of physical effort. They were not just dancing – they were totally living the story; they always managed to have the appropriate expressions on their faces, expressions that fitted into the spirit and story of the dance. Undoubtedly, they were fully involved even though they were at the same time expending a considerable amount of physical effort, and yet the whole dancing appearance was that of effortless movement. The classical tutus made it possible to see the muscles in their legs as they flexed during the complex dancing routine. In some ways, these comments may seem somewhat analytical, but they were my first impressions. The patter of the many pairs of feet in the background was so precise – it was as if a metronome was operating in sympathetic time with the music. Above all, I think I liked watching the dancing, especially the young female dancers, I was fascinated. I could not take my eyes away from them.

Anneliese played the part spectacularly. It was not surprising that she is the prima ballerina assoluta in the Bolshoi Ballet. Occasionally, she would smile in our direction. I am sure we all thought she was glancing at each of us individually, but no, she was smiling at her fiancé, Gabriel. He was part of our party as a personal guest of the First Lady. Anneliese was looking at him, although it was only a fleeting smile, it was the smile of someone very much in love – there was absolutely no doubt about that.

The time passed quickly, and soon I witnessed the overwhelming response of the audience; they were on their feet and would not stop clapping. Eventually, the conductor moved onto the stage, and taking the hand of Anneliese, he brought her forward to the front; the audience was in raptures. Bouquets were being thrown onto the stage, to be collected by the *corps de ballet* dancers. Soon their arms were full and they had to receive additional help from some of the stagehands. The Los Angeles glitterati was very knowledgeable of ballet and the ability of the dancers and loved the spectacle of Swan Lake. Eventually, after nearly thirty minutes the curtain came down, and then as if by magic, I was being introduced to the Russian prima ballerina, Anneliese. She looked beautiful, having made a very rapid change into a delicate pure white dress. She wore very little make-up – just a hint of lipstick, and you could sense that she was experiencing a real high from the adrenaline now flowing within her body. She was holding very tightly onto her American fiancé, Gabriel, making sure that he could not get, away. I have rarely seen two lovers fused by such mutual affection for each other. As you might expect, she was much in demand. The president and his wife where intent in conversation with her, partially in English and partly in German, interpreted by Gabriel. The Secretary of State and his wife and the director of the CIA and his wife were also there. To our pleasure, the First Lady made sure that Jacinta and I were totally involved in the reception.

Rather unusual for me, my mind was now in a whirl. Whilst I couldn't take my eyes off Anneliese, at the same time I was thinking back to the performance during which I could sense that I was being watched. This surely could not be so; who would want to look at me in a box full of US dignitaries. During all the excitement of the audience towards the dancers, for a moment I glanced towards the audience and I thought I got a glimpse of whom? Yes, I think it was Mrs. Lopez, smiling and waving; she was with two young bemused teenage girls, young identical versions of herself. Could it be Mrs. Lopez from Panama – well maybe? After all, this was Los Angeles and Mrs. Lopez lived in Los Angeles. Looking towards her, I instinctively started to wave with both my arms. Jacinta looked at me, wondering what was happening. I could see Mrs. Lopez pointing out to her daughters that she had recognized someone in the presidential box. They also started to wave, jumping up and down in excitement. At that moment, the members of the presidential party started to move and eye contact with Mrs. Lopez was lost.

This incident would not leave my mind; it kept continually coming back to me. No, it could not be her – Mrs. Lopez did not have children. Then, the day before we were to leave Los Angeles, I received a note delivered to the consulate. To my delight, it was from Mrs. Lopez and, yes, she had seen me at the ballet and would like, if it was possible, to meet me and introduce me to her two daughters. She said they had persuaded her to contact me whilst I was still in Los Angeles and, yes, I do have two daughters – was her final remark. Love, Dominique.

So, I was right. It was now well over two decades since we last saw each other, giving her sufficient time to have two daughters. What should I do? In the end, I could not resist telephoning her. A young voice answered, presumably one of her daughters. 'Mama, Mama,' she shouted excitedly. 'Señor Feliciano Solaccio is on the line.' Moments later, I was speaking to Mrs. Lopez.

'I hope you don't mind me writing to you at the consulate, but I didn't want to lose the opportunity of seeing you and it was the only way I knew of contacting you. I saw a photograph of you in the newspaper; it showed all the members of the presidential party, and it mentioned that you were Prime Minister of Colombia. I was stunned! In the end, pressed by my daughters, I decided to risk it and write to you at the Colombian Consulate. It's been a long time since Panama and I have often thought of you. I just had to make contact. My daughters were encouraging me, almost forcing me. At first, I was a little uncertain; you seemed to be with a lady – is she your wife?'

'No, I am not married. That was Jacinta, my political assistant. She ensures I carry out my political duties properly. You are right; I am Prime Minister of Colombia and earlier I was meeting the US president during his visit to Los Angeles. So, you have two daughters?'

'Yes, I have twins, Gabriella and Raffaella. They are sixteen; sadly, my husband was killed in a flying accident more than ten years ago. My daughters look after me and I look after them and it was they, who encouraged me to contact you. I must say, I didn't need much persuading. I often think back to my days in Panama and remember our Spanish lessons. Perhaps we could meet and you could then see my lovely girls?'

'Yes, certainly I did get a glimpse of them at the ballet, and I thought they looked exactly like you.'

'Well, they certainly are much younger.'

'It would be lovely to meet you again; perhaps it would be better if I visited you at your home. Is that possible?'

'It certainly is. How about this afternoon – come and have tea with us. We would love to see you.'

'Yes, I'd love to come. Give me your address – the consulate will help me find it. When?'

'Say, 2:30 p.m.?'

'Fine.'

'I'm sure my girls will be only too keen to meet you and I am certainly looking forward to it, 'till 2.30 then, bye.'

The consulate unmarked car drew up to number 18, on a leafy boulevard on the edges of Los Angeles. Mrs. Lopez and her daughters were out to meet me. We hugged each other whilst the girls looked on with smiles – our first contact was good.

'Feliciano, you look just as you did nearly two decades ago.'

'And you also, Dominique. May I call you Dominique?'

'Yes, please do.'

'You're just the same, only now you have two wonderful daughters who are just perfect images of you. I still can't believe it was you waving to me; what a wonderful experience it turned to be.' Dominique was wearing a pale summer dress – similar to one that I had seen her in by the pool at her Panama villa. Was it by chance or had she deliberately selected it!

'And how wonderful for you to meet the prima donna ballerina, Anneliese.'

'Yes, it was a most enlightening experience being introduced to her and her fiancé, Gabriel. The conversation was mainly in German – a language I fortunately know. Anneliese was happy to talk; she was high with adrenaline from the reception she had just received from a delighted audience. I have never seen anyone quite like that and I have never seen anyone look so much in love – she could barely take her eyes away from Gabriel. She was holding onto him for dear life, not releasing her grasp of his arm. It was only when she was with the president that she released it. Occasionally she spoke in English – with a soft accent, something I had never quite heard before. There was a romantic expression in her eyes all the time.'

Gabriella and Raffaella were fascinated. They never had they seen such a reaction from their mother to a man, other than, of course, their father, who was now beginning to become a distant memory. After a while, the girls realized that they should give their mother some privacy, and left. For a while, we were silent. Then she started to tell me about the last two decades. At first, she was unhappy to leave Panama, but after the twins were born, a busy mother's life took over. Now and then she said she would think back to those happy days, and she often wondered what had happened to me. She could not believe it when she heard that I was now a successful entrepreneur and the prime minister of one of the largest countries of the world, and now once more their paths had crossed.

Her girls were fascinated by our stories of the past and they sensed the possibility of a new romance for their mother. The two girls knew very little about Panama. They were born about two years after Dominique had left, and they didn't seem interested in finding out more. I was uncertain, but I don't believe Dominique ever returned to the villa. I don't think she has been back to Panama. I never really knew the reason why she left in a hurry, and she was not inclined to tell me.

Of course, I would have liked to thank her for the money, but without her address that was impossible. This was the first time that I would be able to thank her. After all, it was her money that was instrumental in setting up my emerald beach stalls – the start of my entrepreneurial career. In the end, I decided to just leave it and not say anything.

For over four hours, we chatted. It was now dark and tomorrow I had an early start. In the morning, Jacinta and I had a planned meeting with the US president's staff, after which we were to return to Bogotá. Before I left, I found myself hugging Gabriella and Raffaella as if they were my daughters, and I felt that Dominique did not want to let me go. I thought I saw an expression in her eyes similar to the one I saw in Anneliese's. We finally parted with promises to keep in contact.

For the next few days, Dominique dominated my thinking. Even Jacinta noticed I was preoccupied. I just had to contact Dominique. Soon I would be going to my villa at Cabo San Lucas, and I wondered if she and the girls would like to join me. They could first visit me in Acapulco and then we could fly to the villa.

Impatiently, I waited for her reply and I couldn't have been more pleased when she said that they would like to come. She said the girls were excited and could hardly believe what was happening.

For the girls, all this was a new exciting experience. When they first caught sight of my villa as our helicopter came into land they were astonished, and finally on the ground, they were overwhelmed, and Dominique was equally stunned. She was visibly excited and was now showing signs to me of much more than just friendship. As we landed, we were greeted by Rosa, Silvia, and José. Gabriella and Raffaella immediately ran up to them, hugging them and kissing them on both cheeks. José certainly was enjoying this new experience. At last, they all must have been thinking, my secluded bachelor life was over, but they hardly expected I was bringing three beautiful girls, home. It looked as if I had hit the jackpot. Inside, Dominique and the girls were shown to their rooms, decorated by Rosa with fragrant fresh flowers. The villa could not have looked better.

For five days we enjoyed the facilities of the villa, swimming in both the sea and in the pool. For me, it was a very unusual experience having two young ladies and Dominique living so close. Dominique had reminded the girls to remain fully dressed at all times. The girls were so much at home that this did not always happen! With a giggle, they would run away. The sound of Shakira's music was constantly heard, and I was beginning to sing to her songs after tuition from the girls.

Each morning, the girls were up at the crack of dawn. They couldn't wait for our morning snorkeling trip to the rocks to see the colorful fish. Dominique stayed in the villa and helped Rosa prepare breakfast. After about an hour of swimming, we would return refreshed and a little tired, ready to tuck into the hot rolls and Blue Mountain coffee. Then we would rest on the terrace, giving Dominique and myself time to chat. Sometimes we would move to the other side of the pool where the girls could not hear – in any event, they were quite happy to give us privacy. They were well aware that their mother had fallen in love, and they appeared to be more than happy with the person she was in love with.

All too quickly, the five days evaporated away and I was on my way back to Bogotá. Dominique and the girls flew back to Los Angeles. Our friendship had now to be conducted by telephone. We would telephone each other every morning and evening and chat for about an hour each time. On each occasion, I would spend some time on the telephone with the girls. I had now become very fond of Gabriella and Raffaella, and I was beginning to think that they were fond of me.

As you would expect, life in Bogotá was pretty hectic. I spent a lot of time with El Presidente and with Jacinta. The infrastructure work was now well underway, and to my great pleasure, I was beginning to see some real signs of hospitals being built and the general health services becoming available. We were fortunate that doctors and nurses from the Philippines and Singapore were able to come to help; they were just the sort of people we needed. I tried to visit my villa as much as I could, and when possible, Dominique and the girls would visit me. Occasionally, Dominique would come on her own. It was a tricky journey for her to make; usually, she had to meet me in Bogotá and we would then fly from there to Cabo San Lucas. Very soon the girls would be going to university and this would then make it easier for Dominique to come and spend some time with me, not only at the villa but also at my apartment in Bogotá. The girls had both been accepted at Stanford University – Raffaella to study computer science and Gabriella, law. My available time for writing novels decreased rapidly, but I managed to spend at least an hour each day, often first thing in the morning. I enjoyed writing and I did not want to stop.

Both Dominique and I were thinking now of making our relationship more permanent. It was quite clear that we were both in love – something that I think was first kindled back in the Panama days. Before I made any plans, I decided to discuss the matter with my friend and old seminarian Cardinal Oscar. Ever since I had left the seminary, I thought I might one day return and continue my studies for the priesthood. I was, therefore, trying hard to cope with a very complex mental state of affairs. Oscar was extremely helpful; he spent a lot of time with me and we went through all the alternatives very carefully. In the end, it was on his advice that I decided to propose to Dominique. She had been well aware of my discussions with Cardinal Oscar and made no attempt whatsoever to influence me and on one occasion accompanied me.

It was with obviously sheer delight that she accepted my proposal of marriage. I had taken the risk to propose in front of Raffaella and Gabriella. Her reply was, 'Yes, please,' and all of us kissed each other for almost ten minutes. I slipped a beautiful emerald and diamond ring on her finger. Marcia had designed and made the ring and it looked just right on her left hand.

A few months later, Cardinal Oscar officiated at our wedding in his private chapel in Cartagena. It was a simple wedding, attended by El Presidente and his wife, all my family, Jacinta, Maria Guadalupe, and some of Dominique's family and friends; Rafaella and Gabriella were our bridesmaids. The Nuptial Mass was in Latin and a quartet from the cathedral sang for us. I can still remember their beautiful singing of Panis Angelicus, the famous St Thomas Aquinas hymn, as we approached Cardinal Oscar for Holy Communion. Our honeymoon was spent at our villa at Cabo San Lucas. Dominique and I had a week together before the girls joined us.

We were now presented with a problem: as prime minister, my time was fully occupied in Bogotá and occasionally in Cartagena. We had no problem with Dominique living with me in my apartment in Bogotá, but what would happen to the girls? Very soon they would be moving to Stanford – where they would take up residence. They could, of course, spend their vacations at Dominique's home in Los Angeles, but if Dominique was living with me, the house would be empty for long periods. For a while, we did not know what to do. Dominique, of course, had her daughters to consider, and for a while, she went back to Los Angeles to look after them and to look after the house. This could only be a temporary arrangement. My busy life did not make things easier. We had no option but to adopt a compromise – the girls should be with their mother at this important time in their life, and we decided that we must simply accept that for periods we would have to live apart. Whenever possible, Dominique and the girls would visit me in either Bogotá or Cabo San Lucas. We simply had to accept that we would be involved in a considerable amount of traveling, and for a while at least, that was the only arrangement possible. I was still in contact with Bunny and Big Daddy, who also lived in Los Angeles, they were able to help look after the girls from time to time. They all got on very well together and the girls were happy to stay with them. To be truthful, I think they all looked forward to their visits.

Absence, indeed, makes the heart grow fonder and we all looked forward to when we were together. In reality, with careful planning, we spent about sixty to seventy percent of our time together, and we loved every minute of it.

Life for me was incredibly different. Suddenly, instead of being essentially someone who would spend a lot of his time alone, I was now spending it with not only one lady friend but three. Both Maria Guadalupe and Jacinta were fascinated by my situation and couldn't help making comments to me about it, usually with a big grin on their faces. It was all very new to me and indeed very exciting. I couldn't wait until we would meet again and I was pleased to see all three girls and I think they had the same view. Suddenly, I had moved from an all masculine world to one which was now essentially feminine. Quite a change! Eleanor secretly asked Jacinta how I was dealing with the situation, again with a big smile on her face, and Cardinal Oscar asked how was I coping – he was most amused by the whole position. My life was now entering a considerable change and no doubt there would be further changes in the future. I would not always be prime minister and the girls would not always be living at home in LA. For a while at least, I was prime minister and the girls would be living at home and that was that.

We were all very happy and that was all that mattered. When this is true there is always a solution to every problem. I certainly now had my fair share of political and domestic intrigue. I had no complaints; it was complicated, but my life with Dominique and the girls couldn't have been better. Never in my wildest dreams did I think anything like that would never occur to me.

We spent as much time as we could at our villa at Cabo San Lucas. Sometimes we would visit beautiful Costa Rica. Costa Rica fully respects nature and indeed was the first country in the world to become carbon neutral.

Epilogue

With help from the International Monetary Fund, it was possible to initiate a program of construction that would develop a fully integrated infrastructure into the vast country of Colombia, after which the economy of the country immediately started to improve. Parallel to this, attention was given to setting up modern educational, welfare and health systems.

El Presidente and Prime Minister Señor Feliciano Solaccio continued to govern Colombia. Alfredo arranged to use the contract with Swiss International Construction for the process of money laundering. For three years, he was very successful, and drug money from abroad paid all the contractors bills, and via corrupt members of the Colombian finance department, equivalent clean IMF money was salted away in Switzerland, Cyprus, Cayman Islands, and Bermuda. Unbeknown to Alfredo's friends, the Swiss International Construction Company started to realize something strange was happening and informed MI6, who, with the help of the CIA, let it run until they knew all who were involved. It took three years to plan a complex process implicating all involved.

Alfredo and his friends are now serving long jail sentences. With an ever-blossoming economy in Colombia, there is no longer a necessity to support this dark economy; the drug business is now rudderless and dying.

Few knew what really happened. Only El Presidente, the Prime Minister, and Señorita Jacinta were privileged to know. The MI6 and CIA did the rest. All the money salted away in offshore accounts has now been returned to the IMF member nations. Even they do not know what really happened – it was termed a dividend on their investment. In actual fact, the drug profits have repaid the entire IMF loan.

A special meeting was held at the White House, and the US president and the UK prime minister dined with El Presidente, Prime Minister Señor Feliciano Solaccio, and Jacinta, together with Petra from the Swiss International Construction Company and the US ambassador to Colombia. No minutes were taken and all felt pleased that the drug nuisance of South and Central America was over. The world is now a safer place to live in.

**

Of course, this is a fictional work. It sets out what might have happened in the fight against the drug trade. The details of what happened during these years will be chronicled at a later date.

Sadly, the truth is that, well into the twenty-first century, the cartels still remain a law unto themselves. Drugs are still grown and transported to all the developed countries of the world. Enormous profits are made, and whilst this remains the case it will be extremely difficult for any government to take effective action. What is more, the cartels have developed drugs to make both distribution and usage easier. Cocaine is now produced in a high state of purity, which means that only very small quantities are now used. Consequently, it is extremely easy for it to be distributed throughout the world. The drugs are essentially produced in South and Central America and the main users are the rich and developed countries of the world, such as the United States of America and the wealthy countries of Europe. If only the underlying story set out in this novel had really taken place, then the world would be a safer place. What is more, their agricultural talents would be used to produce food for the world. How attractive it would have been if the story in this novel had actually occurred.